bayous.

Nowadays he lives his life crime vicariously, through the edgy, fast-paced stories he pens, hoping to entertain readers. When he isn't writing, he's reading, drawing or looking for prospects to train in boxing.

You can find Chris on Facebook **www.facebook.com/OfficialChrisRoy/** and on Twitter @AuthorChrisRoy

Roy delivers on the edge of your seat story-telling with rough edges, crooked cops and a tiny light at the end of the tunnel that is never quite extinguished.
— **Tom Vater,** *journalist, co-founder of Crime Wave Press*

Her Name Is Mercie is a fast furious ride into an inferno of the highest tension you are likely to encounter this year. Where noir meets thriller, toss a coin. Dive in. And unplug your phones, pcs tablets and keep reading deeper and deeper, until the final pages.
— **Richard Godwin,** *author of Apostle Rising*

By the same author

Her Name is Mercie

A Short Story Collection

By Chris Roy

Near To The Knuckle
An imprint of Gritfiction Ltd

Near To The Knuckle
an imprint of Gritfiction Ltd
Rugby
Warwickshire
CV21
www.close2thebone.co.uk

Cover and Interior Design by Craig Douglas

First Printing, 2018

CONTENTS

Her Name Is Mercie

"W asn't that fun?"

"I thought so. Until that half naked harlot climbed on top of that slouch sitting next to you."

"Oh, stop it, Bill. They were just kids in love."

"Love?" Bill growled. He looked at his wife and the car swerved over the center line. "If that's what they call love these days the world is in trouble." His mouth twisted. *Should have asked that slouch to step outside... then* he *would have been in trouble...*

"Watch the road. You know you can't - "

"See good at night anymore. Yes, I know that. We aren't getting old, Dani. We *are* old." He glanced at her.

Dani's eyes shone bright behind her glasses as they passed a streetlight. She clasped her hands in her lap and looked out the windshield, smiling. "It was fun. It was a good picture." She patted Bill's thigh. "And I have no doubt you would have whipped that young man to teach him some respect."

Bill jerked his head toward her, frowning. After a moment he nodded and put both hands on the wheel. His face cocked to the side, part of a smile putting lines in it.

The old Buick floated over the road. The couple enjoyed the quiet hum of the big engine and new tires, watching the fancy new vehicles on the road these days, wondering about the people driving them.

Their daughter had a fancy new car. *Like a little spaceship,* Dani thought. Bill had purchased it new for her birthday last year. She laughed. Bill looked at her and she waved a hand, pressed her lips together. *He would have a fit if he knew she really wanted a big four wheel drive truck...*

Bill sat up straight, turned onto the highway. Racing engines and a booming stereo passed them.

Disgruntled drivers lay on their horns at traffic lights. He braked and scowled at the wheels of an Oldsmobile that came to a grinding stop next to them.

They both looked up as the interior was pierced by the siren and lights of a police car. Flashes of red and blue seemed to fill the car. Disorienting beams bounced off the roof, seats and dashboard, the police cruiser racing up behind them.

"Lord have mercy, Bill! Pull over so they can go around."

He grumbled, nervous hands turning the wheel. The cruiser pulled in behind them.

"Hell is wrong?" Bill squinted at his side view mirror. The policemen were already out and approaching. And their guns were drawn. "*Hell* is wrong?" He pointed at the glove box. "Insurance card, Dani."

She leaned forward, looking closely at the latch. The lights were blinding. She adjusted her glasses and they fell on the floorboard. "Durn it. Dropped my glasses." She felt around, hunched over.

Bill leaned over the console and stuck his long arm under her leg, fingers brushing over the floor mat. "You find them? I can't find them."

"No."

"I told you to get - "

"A cord. Yes, Bill. For Heaven's sake. I'll get a cord for my durn glasses." She grunted. "If I can find them."

The officers approached and saw two forms bent over trying to grab something under the passenger seat. They stopped at the back of the Buick. One of them called for the driver and passenger to show their hands. The search under the seat continued, movements frantic.

Moving wide apart, the officers took aim at the

doors on both sides, steadying their hands, hearts racing. Red, yellow and blue refracted on the recently washed Buick, flickered on their uniforms. Cars blew past, wind pulsing from heavy traffic. Both officers shouted repeated demands for the driver and passenger to show their hands.

The passenger sat up. Light reflected from an object in her hand.

The officers opened fire.

***

The door chimed. Mercie glanced over to see a woman and three kids enter. She finished typing, smiled and handed over a customer's debit card and receipt. The short Latino man thanked her in accented English and left.

The woman and kids - two boys and a girl - moved to the back of the store. Mercie's lips thinned as the boys went to the candy aisle, ignoring their mother's demands to stay close and behave. They were maybe eight and ten, the age where young boys' - if it's in them - inner larcenous monkey comes out.

Large mirrors were positioned high at the back of the store, above the soda cooler. One showed a clear view of the candy aisle. The other showed the left wall. Lunchables, microwaveable burritos, hotdogs, burgers and such were displayed there in more coolers. A surprising number of drug addicts stole the Lunchables. Mercie didn't understand why until she got lucky one day and caught one. The man actually returned the Lunchable instead of bolting out the door. He dropped his head, scratched it and muttered, "The dope man buys 'em. Gives a dub for five. Sometimes a double up."

His response answered her question but left her even more confused. And curious. Unfortunately, the man realized what he was saying and to whom, then he *did* bolt out of the store. Pissed Mercie off; she had more questions.

Was he high? She tapped a finger on her lips.

Keeping an eye on the mirrors she checked the cash register's display, the receipt stubs, tidying up. She had no help today so restroom breaks were difficult. She always had to lock the store and run to the ladies room, get her business done, and run back to open again. There were always customers at the gas pumps or peeking through the doors when she returned.

She looked at the empty Coke bottle under the counter and said, "Brilliant."

The boys were whispering together in front of boxes of Snickers, M&Ms, and a small selection of baseball cards. One of them squatted and grabbed a few pieces of 5¢ gum from a plastic bucket, walked to the counter. The other boy watched him go, turning a few times to look at the back of the store.

Mercie tried not to sigh as the boy put the gum and some nickels on the counter. "Is that all?"

"Yes, ma'am." He smiled. He was missing some front teeth, had freckles and plump cheeks. Mercie would have thought him adorable if the larcenous monkey wasn't lurking behind his eyes. He pointed behind her. "Do you have any baseball card price guides?"

She didn't turn around so he kept pointing and asking about other things. She opened the register, made the sale, and dropped the nickels in the drawer. She glanced up and saw the other boy sticking something in his pants' waist, pulling his shirt over it. He made a grab for candy bars and dropped one. He looked up and saw Mercie staring at him.

The phone next to the register rang. The boy in front of her was chewing his gum and picking through a display rack on the counter. She kept an eye on the other thief and snatched up the phone. *I'll ask the mother to search them and pay for the items. If they lie...*

"Thank you for calling *Stop and Shop*. This is Mercie, how may I help you?"

"This is Chief Dexter Perez of the Biloxi Police Department. Mercie Hillbrook?"

"This is she. I was just about to call you guys. Well, maybe."

"Is that right? Pertaining to what?"

She pictured a gray buzz cut and short gray beard over a stout frame, large dark hand making the phone look tiny. "You first," she said. Her eyes moved to the woman approaching with the little girl in tow.

"Okay. Miss Hillbrook, there's only one way I know how to make these calls. *Direct.* The reason I'm calling is to notify you that your presence is needed at the county morgue, at fifteen hundred hours, to identify the bodies of a Mister William Hillbrook and a Miss Danielle Hillbrook." He breathed into the phone. "There was an accident today during a routine traffic stop. On behalf of the Biloxi Police Department, Miss Hillbrook, you have our deepest sympathies and condolences."

Mercie tilted her head, held the phone on her shoulder and rang up the customer. The woman spoke about her hectic day, oblivious to the phone. The girl, on the woman's hip now, played with her mother's hair and giggled at the hand failing to stop her game. Mercie stared at the boys that walked slowly towards the door. But she didn't really see them.

The out-of-focus customers became a blur, the woman's words a high-pitched ringing. Disembodied hands appeared in front of her and closed the register, handed change over the counter. The fingers were long, nails short.

A small tattoo wrapped around the left wrist: a black cat with green eyes.

A vibration persisted on the side of her head. *A voice?* Her mouth moved with the thought. She looked at her hands, the floor. At her cheap Skechers. It was like a low-res video with no sound.

The customers blurred into the background, door chiming open, closed. Something cracked against the counter. Her eyes were drawn to movement below, the phone receiver bobbing on the twisted cord, knocking into the lower shelf.

Pain flared from her stomach. All at once her vision focused, the ringing in her ears vanished and the low-res video became her reality. She held out her hands and tried to stop them from shaking. Biting back a scream she clenched her hands into tight fists and bolted from the store.

***

God, they look so old. Tears welled, nose running. Mercie sniffed and wiped with a tissue the assistant coroner gave her. She looked at the officers standing behind her and nodded. Two of them walked away looking at paperwork.

Looking at her parents she sent up a silent prayer, thankful their faces hadn't been mutilated. She immediately felt guilty. They were dead. Concern for how they looked dead was selfish. Her lip pushed out. *They look stately. Mom looks regal as ever. But God they look old, and very… dead.*

She pressed her palms together, finger tips under her nose, trying to imagine their peace in Heaven. Smiling, she could hear her mom now, chiding her for not going to church or praying anymore. "Came back from college with a degree in atheism" is how she described Mercie's master's in biology.

She smiled wide and those built-up tears sprang across her cheeks.

Memories she once enjoyed feeling took her to a different place. One of pain. Cold fear clutched at her heart. She had to force herself to breath.

"Miss Hillbrook."

She blinked and let the tears run. Her eyes moved over the sheets covering her parents. She wanted to see the gunshot wounds… but she didn't. She looked back at their gray faces. She couldn't breathe and had to look away. She froze and stared at the stainless steel freezer that contained the Grim Reaper's Lunchables. She didn't recognize the person staring back in the reflection.

Her hair was light brown and long like her mom's. Though it looked like it hadn't been brushed. Ever. Her eyes were large, sad blue things like her dad's, with thick dark eyebrows that were probably, in her opinion, the sole reason she was single. Her face was round with a large nose. But cute. Most of the time. Whenever she wasn't sad.

Or in a sudden homicidal rage.

"Miss Hillbrook," Chief Perez said. "Once again, on behalf of the - "

"Murderers," Mercie snapped. She spun around. Chief Perez had the short gray beard like she imagined, but had long curls around his ears, on his forehead. He had tiny eyes behind tinted prescription glasses. She hated his voice on the phone. Hated him even more in person. "On behalf of a bunch of murderers, you mean?"

Chief Perez glanced at the bodies. He fumbled in his pocket, keys jingling, pulled out a tin of mints and put one in his mouth. He took a breath and chose his words with care. "Miss Hillbrook. What happened was tragic. Nothing can change that. But it was not intentional. It was a routine stop and the officers were following procedure. There's been a lot of violence against law enforcement around the country, especially against patrol officers. Our procedures are done so for the safety of our officers."

"Uh-huh. I suppose on the highway with all the traffic and distracting lights your officers thought my parents were young black guys in a stolen car."

The assistant coroner cleared his throat. Chief Perez nodded and he pushed the tables with the bodies back into the freezer. He secured the latches and left. Chief Perez chose not to respond to her accusation.

Mercie ground her teeth, looking at the Grim Reaper's Lunchable cooler. She would never see her mom or dad again.

She lost her equilibrium and staggered. Chief Perez caught hold of her shoulder, elbow. Her shaking hands turned into tight fists.

"You okay?"

For an answer, she looked at him and punched as hard as she could.

***

The Ace bandage was too tight. Her fingers were tingling. And she couldn't shake the image of her fist curving next to his face, smashing into the steel cabinet next to him.

As she waited for the Regions executive to get off the phone she massaged her forearm and looked around the office. Weary from the funeral and dealing with her aunts and uncles who showed up like scavengers, she had to squint to see the framed diplomas and fancy certificates on the wall behind the bitch on the phone.

Lady knows my parents were murdered. Knows how serious this is…

She eased her wrapped hand from the arm of the chair, placed it in her lap. She tried to wiggle the numb fingers. Wincing, she drummed her boots on the floor. *Because* that *was a good idea.*

The phone was placed in its cradle. "Mercie Hillbrook."

"You said that already. Earlier. Before I told you everything my parents worked for their entire lives could be lost." She straightened in the chair, smoothed wrinkles from her skirt.

The executive - Page MacIntyre, her nameplate read - moved her mouth into something resembling a smile. She rested her elbows on the desk, interlaced her fingers. Her short red bangs moved as she talked around her hands. "Miss Hillbrook, foreclosure isn't certain. However, you are not listed on the mortgage application, and consequently were not approved as a successor. After reviewing your personal account records I can safely say you will not be approved if you file an application for succession." She moved her face to the other side of her hands and gave her fake smile again. "Is there anyone - "

"No. And you know that. There's no one. No one but a bunch of greedy, evil ass-hats that call themselves 'bankers'."

"This conversation has become inappropriate." Page pushed her chair back, swiveled and rolled over in front of a desktop PC. She grabbed the mouse. "Miss Hillbrook, here at Regions we honor loan agreements to the letter. When a customer is no longer able to honor *their* side of the agreement, nor have they taken steps to insure a succession, then that agreement becomes void. Voiding an agreement can result in automatic foreclosure. In this case, unfortunately, it did." The computer screen lit up her face, eyes dark with smokey-style makeup. "We are in the *banking* business, Miss Hillbrook. If we went against our policy, for anyone, we could not remain in business and hundreds of citizens now and thousands in the future would not attain their dreams of owning homes, vehicles and their own businesses."

"You cold-hearted bit - " Mercie swallowed that last word. Page turned and lifted one perfectly plucked brow, head tilted. Mercie stood slowly and smiled. Smoothed her skirt. She relaxed and said, "You're right, Miss MacIntyre. Thank you for seeing me today."

She left the office. Walked around the teller counter and ignored two men who snickered at her from a line of waiting customers.

She didn't own a car. And her parents' only car was at a police impound full of bullet holes. She stopped next to her scooter, grabbed the helmet off the handle bar. Winced as the chin strap clicked under her chin. The Honda 125cc fired right up. She sat on it wishing it was a big beast of a motorcycle so she could rev the engine and leave a long, pissed-off burnout.

She made sure her skirt was tucked and maneuvered out onto the road, little engine sputtering. She stopped at Sears and went into the sporting goods section. Made a purchase and left the store.

Ten minutes later she was leaning into the curves of a sub-division jam-packed with new houses. She stopped in front of one, turned off the scooter, put it on its kickstand and marched up to the front door. She was aware she still had the helmet on, though had no idea why.

She rang the doorbell.

A minute later the door opened and a sixty-something lady in a fluffy white robe stood there. She frowned at the helmet. "Yes? Hello."

Mercie pulled a gun from behind her back and

stuck the barrel in the woman's face. "Keys! Give me your car keys!"

She tried to shut the door. Mercie lunged forward, stuck her arm inside. The door smashed her Ace wrapped hand and she screamed. She shoved the door open with all her weight. The lady nearly toppled over, catching herself on a closet doorknob, as Mercie barged in pointing the gun again. It shook as she growled, *"Keys!"*

"There. They're over there!" She indicated a key rack on a wall in the kitchen. She held up her hands, shallow breaths loud.

The big house was air conditioned, which gave Mercie pause when sweat stung her eyes. She wiped her face on her sleeve. Jerked the gun towards the kitchen. The woman hurried over and got the keys. They rattled as she handed them over.

Mercie looked at the woman and tried to say why she did what she did. What came out was a frustrated gurgling noise. She groaned, acted like she wanted to swat the lady in the face with the gun. She spun and stomped out of the house.

The Impala's door handle was hot in the afternoon sun. Mercie climbed in, slammed the door and became aware of how fast she was breathing. The keys rattled, ignition key punching in the slot. The engine made the pedals vibrate under her boots. She fumbled for reverse and pushed the accelerator a little too hard.

A crunching boom jacked up the rear of the car. It slammed down and over the Honda, front end doing the same, dragging the little scooter out into the street. She looked at her poor scooter, pouty lip sticking out. "Brilliant," she said, shifting into drive. She bared her teeth and growled, "What the *fuck?*"

This time she was able to leave a long, pissed-off

burnout.

***

The bank was almost closed. She reversed into a handicapped parking space and left the engine running. As she got out the guys that were looking at her with judgmental humor earlier were getting into a nearby car. She pointed the gun at them and felt a thrill of satisfaction when their eyes widened. Unintelligible shouts could be heard inside their car as it raced past.

She shut the Impala's door and stalked up the path to the entrance. On the highway behind her brakes locked up, tires skidding, a second before the men's car was T-boned by a monster SUV.

Mercie, holding the lobby door open, watched smoke rise from the wreck. Her eyebrows stood up. She turned, remembering the gun in her hand and her purpose for having it. Rage replaced the astonishment as soon as she saw the tellers, the offices on the other side.

The tread of her boots gripping the carpet was the only sound inside once the tellers noticed her. One ducked under the counter. Another was on a phone, glancing at the door. Mercie realized they heard and maybe saw the wreck and had called emergency services.

At this point who cares? She tried a menacing look, which wasn't hard, pointing the gun at the woman on the phone. The modelesque blonde, a perfect Size Two, hung up the phone and held up her hands.

Mercie looked at the woman's waist again. Her finger tightened on the trigger. "Money! All of it! Put it in a bag and hand it over!" She waved the gun at the other tellers. "All of you! Bag the cash and put it on the counter or I will shoot you in the waist. Face. I will shoot you in the *face!"*

The tellers moved quickly, holding small wastebasket liners, stuffing bound stacks of cash inside them.

Mercie looked over her shoulder and saw her reflection in the glass door. She still had the helmet on. And it looked ridiculous.

The rage continued to burn in her chest, though she could no longer hold the menace on her features.

Three bags were on the counter. The fourth teller was crying, shaking so bad she kept dropping money. Mercie didn't wait on her. Snatching up the bags, she tried to yell, "Hands up! Get back!" but only managed a confused expulsion of spit. She shook the gun and snarled like she meant to do that. Turned and stomped out of the bank.

The door hissed shut. She squinted around, scared. Then she remembered the Impala, saw it right in front of her and exhaled. Opening the door she squeaked as a boy sat up in the seat. In his hands were the car's stereo, wiring harness stretched out of the dashboard, and a large screwdriver. He was Asian, probably Vietnamese, had short black hair, wide-set epicanthic eyes and teeth that needed braces. Grease stains spotted his tee shirt and jeans.

They locked eyes. Hers moved to study him, the screwdriver. His moved to the bags, the gun in her Ace wrapped hand.

He laughed, fell over the console.

"What? Kid... *What?* Dude, get out!" She waved the gun.

He laughed again. "That's only a BB gun." He slid the stereo back into the dashboard.

"So?" She stood up straight, groaned and leaned into the car, stuck the gun right in his face. "It still stings…"

He swallowed. Looked into her eyes. Sirens pierced the traffic discord, making both of them look. He motioned for her to hand him the bags. For whatever reason, she did. He scrambled over the seat, into the back. She got in, shifted. The door slammed as she left a satisfying burnout across the parking area.

As she was turning out onto the side road police cars raced into the lot from the highway. She looked up, saw a trail of smoke following her in the rearview and cursed. Two police cars fishtailed out onto the street behind them, engines roaring, more tire smoke joining hers.

She tried to grip the wheel with both hands. Confused, fractured fingers slid the gun over the top of it. The cat's eyes on her wrist seemed to mock her. Turning onto Highway 90 she shouted, "God, that was brilliant… I'm so *stupid*. Ugh!"

Traffic was bumper-to-bumper, every stoplight overworked. The Impala did a drunken shake, thudding over the curb, onto the beach parking lane. The engine revved, her boot pressed hard on the accelerator, pushing her back into the seat.

Bouncing over a drainage grate, the boy's hands disappeared from next to her shoulder, his arms and knees banging on the floorboard. He sucked in a breath. *"Cac! Du ma!"*

The sun cooked the sand and water, degrading the skin and eyes of the few people enjoying the beach. Plumes of sand rose from behind the police cars in her rearview mirror. A strange calm steadied her breathing. Her hands stopped shaking and sensed the road, the wheels and engine. She flipped the visor down, swerved around a row of parked cars and sideswiped a small gray pickup in a line at a light. The sudden impact made the boy curse in

Vietnamese again. His hands reappeared, dark eyes peering over the seat. "Don't crash," he said.

"Duh."

She braked, a police cruiser only feet from the Impala, and, unable to see the lights, turned into an intersection. Horns were loud on both sides. Something clipped the rear-end, knocking the Impala sideways. Mercie meant to hit the brake, stomping the gas pedal, smashing into a passing truck, metal screeching, sliding past. She screamed. So did the boy.

Her boot stayed pressed on the pedal. She gasped and held her breath as she realized they were about to go over railroad tracks. A quaking boom of cars colliding at the intersection behind them made her flinch.

The calm she enjoyed a moment ago was vanquished.

Screaming filled the car again, front-end compressing, ramping the tracks. Queasy vertigo spread from her stomach, cheating gravity, launching up her throat, head nearly smacking the wheel on the landing. Her vision came back. She looked at her boot and made it ease up. She spun to look for the police and saw a crooked smile instead.

"That was fun!" The boy was smiling and laughing. It made her smile and laugh.

She looked over his head, saw only one police car and decided it was progress. "Woo-*hoo!*"

The boy mimicked her triumphant shout.

Nearly ramming into a casino shuttle killed the moment.

The road became clear. Before she could take advantage the police car plowed into the Impala, spinning it. Instinctively, she over-compensated. Her lack of experience only made the car spin faster in the wrong direction. Skidding, they crashed to a stop against a row of parked cars. Pressed against the window, her moan fogged the glass.

Tire tread barked outside the passenger door, police car sliding to a stop, light bar throwing crazy colors and flashes all over the street, businesses on either side. Small beams in the cruiser's grill blinked into the Impala's interior.

Mercie slammed a fist on the wheel. She looked at the cars smashed up against her door. Looked at the police car. An image of her parents being shot to death, how she envisioned the brutal absurdity must've happened, and heat flared from the pit of her stomach to her face. Tears blurred her eyes. She shouted her parents' names, pointed her gun at the cruiser and pulled the trigger.

The gun coughed. The BB rebounded off the window and struck her cheek.

The boy popped up. "Did you get him?"

Mercie, hand on her cheek, dropped the gun and rested her head on the wheel. "No," she sighed.

***

The worst thing about jail, Mercie thought, was having to shower in front of two dozen other women. The fact that she was facing twenty years for bank robbery, ten for stealing the Impala, with maybe another five for evading arrest - and would owe around a million dollars in restitution for property damage and hospital bills - wasn't anywhere in her awareness as she looked at the tiled square in the corner of the dayroom. There was no curtain. Nowhere to even put a soap dish or the tiny bottle of questionable shampoo they gave her. There was a corroded showerhead. There was a button that, from what she had witnessed so far, was a roulette that either scalded you or froze you.

And, there was a hook.

Mercie hung her towel on the hook. Thought about it and took it off. She hung her pants, shirt, underwear and *then* the towel, thinking she made a smart move. Until she looked around for a place to put the clothes she had on. The floor was a wet, nasty thing, and guaranteed an automatic trip to the laundry for anything that touched it.

She double-checked the clothes on the hook.

She glanced around. The dayroom had four cells, each with a bunk bed and a third mattress on the floor. Low fiberglass bunks lined the walls and stuck out from the spaces between cells. A steel picnic table, once blue, chipped with graffiti on top of graffiti, had a card game going on one end, and four women sitting at the other end watching *Maury*. A small TV was mounted high on the wall behind Plexiglas. The women were all young, a couple her age, some younger. *And they're all thinner and better looking, even in these stupid orange uniforms.*

But no one was watching her.

Confused still, she took off her clothes and placed them on the driest spot on the edge of the tiled square. They let her keep the Ace bandage. She unwrapped it and almost fell over trying to keep her feet off the floor and on the stiff foam shower shoes. The hard rubber thongs felt as if they'd slice into her toes. She held an arm over her breasts as she leaned over, pulled them on tight.

She lost the shower roulette. It was scalding. The steaming water hit the top of her feet and she hopped back, grabbing the hook. Someone behind her laughed. She didn't know if it was from her scalded hop, the way she jiggled all over, or from Maury announcing the results of a lie detector test. She felt her face redden and turned toward the shower.

There was no way she could get under the water. It seemed hot enough to sterilize surgical equipment. And no way was she going to stand there and wait for it to turn cold.

Soaking her wash cloth, she lathered soap on it, scrubbed thoroughly from face to feet, and used it to rinse off the soap. She had to let the cloth cool each time she soaked it.

Thirty minutes later she sat on her bunk, dressed in orange over white, contemplating various medications to avoid a future of recurring shower nightmares.

She looked at the TV but wasn't watching it. *The Jerry Springer Show* was on. Her eyes moved to the card game. It had become lively. Three black girls talked with animated gestures, making their individual points by slamming cards on the table. Mercie smiled. They were passing time doing something they obviously enjoyed.

Mercie looked at the girl dealing a new hand. She was *Mexicana*, spoke quietly, and never smiled. She looked dangerous, looked like a seasoned convict; the tattoos on her arms and neck had a gang theme, and her uniforms were neatly pressed from being folded and placed under her mattress.

Using the toilet was nearly as bad as the shower. There was one in every cell, but the cells were always full of people. At night one cell was left open in case the girls in the dayroom needed to use the toilet. Problem was, the girls in the cell were sleeping. Waking and asking them to leave while she used the toilet was out of the question. She just had to go in and use it.

Going to pee in the stainless steel bowl sounded like a high pressure hose in the confines of the quiet cell. If that didn't wake everyone - and embarrass her to the brink of suicide - flushing did.

A girl no more than eighteen told her the "proper" way of taking a deuce was to flush right away and keep flushing until she finished. "Courtesy flushes," she said, giving Mercie a confused look. "Ain't you in here for armed robbery?"

"Yeah…"

"Better get used to it, then."

Doing her business in the daytime, with no one in the cell, twisted around so she could flush at the same time, took some getting used to. Doing it at night with a girl laying on the floor three feet from her exposed ass was something she hoped to never get used to.

She spent the first week laying on her bunk reading old magazines and a novel. *Shank* was written by a guy in prison. He escaped Parchman's old supermax, and the main character in his book escaped Parchman, too, though differently. She read the entire thing in a day.

Hmm… She closed the book after reading about the author again.

The *clunk* of heavy steel drew her out of her reverie. The zone door whined open on its track. A deputy sheriff stepped in. Tall with narrow shoulders and wide hips, her gun belt creaked as she put a hand on the empty holster and read from a notepad.

"Mercie Hillbrook." Her tone projected authority, eyebrows furrowing. She looked around at the girls, distaste evident.

Mercie didn't answer immediately. She felt anger at the deputy. Then amazement; she was usually the one judging those type of girls.

Scowling - at herself this time - she got up from her bunk, slid into her shower shoes and followed the deputy into the hallway, door clunking shut. She looked at the deputy's butt. *If I had my boots on...*

"You stole my wife's car." Chief Perez stood next to the control room, hands planted on the sides of his ample belly. He shook his head. "Robbed my wife, is what you did."

Mercie unclasped her hands and held up her chin. "I did," she said with the air of accomplishing a life goal. Her mouth and eyes tightened. "Because you weren't home to steal yours."

He wasn't expecting that kind of response. His small eyes showed uncertainty behind his glasses. His wide nose flared once. "What happened to you, lady?"

She shifted her weight on one foot and stared back. *You know damn well what happened,* she almost shouted.

The deputy got a nod from him and walked back into the cell blocks looking at her notepad. Electronic locks buzzed, huge key rings bumped gun belts as deputies went about their tasks. Chief Perez sighed, tapping out on the stare down. Turning to the side he motioned with his head for her to follow him.

The visitation room was long and narrow, steel stools anchored to the floor in front of a steel counter with steel partitions and Lexan. They sat together in the inmates' side, a stool between them. He shifted several times and wouldn't look directly at her, unsettled from the tiny hard stool and from whatever he came to talk about.

She wasn't uncomfortable. She was murderous.

"It's not good enough." She almost spit on him.

Surprise touched his face. "How do you know I'm here to offer you anything?" He chuckled. "In my thirty-six years with the police department I've never met a criminal like you. Know what that tells me?" He didn't let her respond. "Tells me you're not a criminal." He tapped a knuckle on the stool between them.

"It's. Not. Good. Enough." She rapped her injured knuckles on the stool. Pain registered on her face as deepening anger. She unwrapped the Ace, balled it up and stuck it in her back pocket. *Stupid... useless... ugh!*

He leaned with a hand on his knee, smoothed his beard with the other. "People facing a few years can afford to have your attitude. But you are facing a few *decades*. You can't afford to pass up any help. *Any* help. Because of what happened... I was there when you had to identify the bodies of your parents - "

"Who would *still be alive* if your officers hadn't *murdered* them!"

He stuck his palms out, pumping them at her. Sticking a finger behind his glasses, he scratched an eye. "Let's not get crazy, uh, carried away, Miss Hillbrook. 'Murdered' is not at all what happened. So let's get past that. I'm here to offer you a deal, one never given to anyone with your crimes."

"And I said it's not good enough." She folded her arms.

"Not good enough, how? What else do you want? You robbed a bank, lady. You robbed my wife at gunpoint, then destroyed her car and half the city! You can't keep the money, and you owe my wife a damn car!"

She leaned forward, placing her hands flat on the stool. Their breathing filled the pause. Her words oscillated with quiet intensity. "How much time are the officers going to get?"

"Excuse me? *Time?*"

"How much will the police department be fined for killing my parents? So far, the only person that has truly lost something is me."

He blew out a breath and ticked off on his fingers.

"The bank lost. Customers, mostly, and the money you took, which magically disappeared."

The money? He's playing an interrogation game. She frowned but kept the thought to herself.

"Innocent bystanders, good citizens driving home from work, also lost. Their vehicles wrecked, time in hospitals, lost time at work and home. And my wife." He pointed at her. "And *me,* because of the way she lost it! Dammit." He stood and paced around the stools.

She recalled the terror on his wife's face and battled her feelings. She stood and rubbed her butt while he was turned away. "Were the officers even suspended?"

He spun around. "Yes! They were. And this isn't a negotiation any longer. I came here out of respect for what happened to innocent people. But I see you are not innocent at all! Revenge, Miss Hillbrook, is a crime. *Premeditated* crime. Take it to trial and I can guarantee you will be punished to the full extent of the law."

She moved back as he brushed past. He stopped at the door, facing it, hand on the knob. "What happened to the money, Miss Hillbrook?"

***

Everyone was sleepy-eyed, lining up at the door to get their breakfast trays. Except for two girls. Their eyes were wide open and red. From talking all night. Several girls, including Mercie, glowered at them, thinking how nice it would be to see their entire faces red. From multiple slaps.

The trays - weird because they were thick plastic *and* an ugly beige - were passed through a slot in the zone door by an old man in green and white striped pants. The trustee hollered, "Trays!" every time he grabbed them from a new stack. The heavy duty cart also had a plastic keg full of coffee. Mercie grabbed her tray and passed her cup out the slot. The trustee took it, wordless, set it on the cart with the others.

She sat on her bunk, tray on her lap. Warm condensation soaked through her pants and she resisted pouting. She meant to put a towel under the tray. *Brilliant morning to me...*

There were no locker boxes to keep clothes, toiletries and food in. Only brown paper bags from the canteen. Reaching under her bunk she grabbed a spork and a length of tissue from a rolled down bag. She looked at her tray and stabbed a little gray circle that, according to the menu taped by the door, was "sausage". The spork bent. The gray circle just squished a little. Forcing calm, she set the utensil down, picked up the sausage and ate it in one quick bite.

She looked at the spork, glad it didn't work, glad she didn't have to experience that more than once.

The eggs and grits were more cooperative. She ate, drank her milk.

The tray issuing done, the coffee was passed in a cup at a time. This morning, the Mexican girl volunteered to hand them out, looking at each cup to see who it belonged to. Everyone marked their cup. Mercie had scratched a tiny "M.H." on it with a staple. She thought the effort was wasted since she hadn't drank a single cup yet. The "coffee" was dark brown and hot. The resemblance ended there.

She stacked her tray next to the door, got her cup and thanked the girl. She walked over to the shower, sniffing the coffee. It was the same as yesterday and the days before. Drove her nuts. She ached for a cup of good coffee, and couldn't believe she kept getting it every morning expecting it to be different, expecting whoever was playing the joke to quit and pass out the real caffeine.

Poised over the shower drain, a hand touched her shoulder. She nearly spilt it. The Mexican girl pointed at the cup and held up a soda bottle half-full of the crud. Mercie smiled and handed her the cup. The girl, Juanita, poured it in the bottle, returned the cup and walked away.

Mercie wanted to ask how she planned to drink it - there were no microwaves - but Juanita's demeanor seemed to ban chit-chat of any kind.

"Get ready for cleanup!" a deputy announced on the PA system. "Cleanup time! Everyone will participate."

Three times a week an assortment of brooms, mops, brushes and buckets were pushed onto the zone. There were some who didn't participate in 'cleanup'. Though they would have if given the chance; some of the girls stood at the door waiting on cleanup, and pushed each other out of the way to get the good broom or brush.

Mercie folded her mattress in half, set her bags on the bunk and tried to stay out of the way. The control tower had turned on some music. The PA system was overwhelmed by an R&B station, speaker popping and buzzing on the bass notes. As the zone filled with the scent of detergents and heavy duty cleaner, girls sang Johnny Taylor, mounds of dust and hair blithely swept to the center of the floor. Two girls stood on top of a bunk dancing.

Mercie walked over and sat on the table, feet on the bench, facing the cells. Inside the far right cell, Juanita squatted in front of the toilet holding a string with her coffee bottle attached to the end. Underneath, perched on the edge of the stainless toilet, was a burning milk carton. The flames licked around the plastic bottle, shrinking it. Fascinated, Mercie watched the carton burn to ashes. Before it went out Juanita used it to light another carton, swatting the ashes into the water. She twisted the top on the bottle to release pressure, tightened it, lowered it into the flames.

Mercie's eyes had pinpricks of fire, lost in thought. *How did she light it?*

Juanita noticed she had an audience, stood and pulled the door closed.

An argument broke out by the shower. The singing stopped. Two girls had a large can of Ajax between them. White powder shot up from their hands every time one snatched at it. Between their feet lay a large brush, shower running behind them, wetting their pants, arms and hair.

Everyone sensed what would happen next and encircled them. The combatants shouted horrible things about each other, throwing wild slaps, grabbing hair and raking at faces.

"You ain't about that life!" screeched one, smacking at the other.

The Ajax was crushed on the tile. The zone reverberated with laughter, cheers and taunts.

The zone door slid open, several deputies rushing in with cans of pepper spray held out like pistols. They were ignored by most, who continued watching the spectacle, blood drawn on both fighters now.

Mercie, still sitting on the table, winced when one of the deputies jumped in between the wild swings and caught an elbow in the face. The deputy responded by emptying an entire can of pepper spray in all directions. The orange vapor scattered the crowd, but there was nowhere to run. In seconds everyone was hacking, coughing, noses running, eyes tightly shut and burning. One girl wheezed about having asthma. The deputies ignored her, running into the hallway, pepper fog trailing their coughing.

***

Deputies in gas masks escorted every girl to the lockdown cellblock and strip-searched them. The two fighters were locked in separate cells, still covered in pepper spray, one screaming about scratches on her face burning. Mercie looked around at the others while putting her clothes back on. She noticed - *felt* - a wide range of emotions in the room.

Nearly everyone had inhaled it. Mercie fought a strong cough. Some had orange stains on skin, hair and clothes. If washed, it only spread. It wasn't going anywhere. And a shower would make it worse. "Make it cover your whole body," a girl with a star tattooed on her cheek said, sneezing.

The water atomizes it. Mercie glanced at the shower, considering the agony of scalding water combined with the pepper spray.

The foul atmosphere wasn't helped by news of the large group of deputies shaking down their cellblock.

An eternity later a deputy standing by the door told them to get up and walk back to their zone without talking. The hallway was freezing, air conditioner going non-stop. Men stood in the windows of neighboring cellblocks, waving and shouting things. It made Mercie glad the walls were thick. Some of the girls waved and shouted back. The deputy trailing the group promised to issue write-ups for disobeying her orders.

Mercie stopped at the foot of her bunk. She rubbed her eyes and groaned. *Wonderful...* Her mattress was hanging off on the floor, sheet balled up on top of brown bags, clothes and hygiene items she was sure weren't hers. She turned to search through the chaos. Curses and homicidal threats directed at the deputies came from the cells. Patches of orange, thickest by the shower, tracked all over the floor, into every cell. An orange boot print unfolded as she pulled on her sheet.

Juanita walked over. Smirked at the boot print. It was the first time Mercie had seen her express humor... first time seeing her express *anything*.

Some of the dread eased and Mercie felt herself mirroring Juanita's smirk. "I know, right?" She pulled at her uniform top. "As if there wasn't enough of this gorgeous color, they had to print orange patterns on our beds, too."

Juanita cleaned and filled the mop bucket with hot soapy water. They put their sheets in to soak and helped clean the zone again. And again. The walls had to be scrubbed numerous times. Mercie got to help this time, but only because no one wanted to clean the shower. She knew why, and couldn't believe she had volunteered.

As soon as she turned on the shower, steam rose and engulfed her with a fresh dose of pepper spray.

***

The cleaning and washing went on through the night. Mercie lay in bed with a roll of toilet tissue next to her, sniffling, eyes closed. She burned all over. It seemed she had just fallen into an exhausted sleep when someone called her name.

"Hillbrook! Get ready for court."

Her swollen eyes unstuck, blinking. A deputy stood at the end of her bunk looking at a sheaf of papers. She mumbled an acknowledgement and sat up.

Dressed in her still-wet uniform, hair pulled back, shower shoes on, she was escorted to the front of the jail and told to stand in line with girls who looked as bad as she did. Deputies were putting restraint gear on them. Mercie turned toward the wall, held on to it and lifted each foot for a deputy to shackle. Turned front and tried not to cringe as the deputy put a chain around her waist and locked it and cuffed her hands to the chain.

Friendly banter between the deputies and some of the girls surprised Mercie. The morning shift was far less strict with 'fraternizing'.

The van ride to the courthouse was uneventful. "Just a bunch of bitches hauled in front of a judge who don't give a shit," a girl in the back said. The building on the narrow street appeared to be far too small for so many people. Transport vans and police cruisers dominated the parking areas, their plainness accentuating the high-end styles of luxury sedans and SUVs owned by suits with law degrees.

A seagull cawed overhead, a winged silhouette in the blinding sun. Mercie squinted at it, looking out the van's open door. A deputy helped her get out. Shackles rattled, digging into her ankles. Another deputy kept a close eye on the group, making them stand in two lines. They hobbled across the road.

The roar of the nearby highway and Gulf pushed at them, breeze rustling hair and making their baggy uniforms flap. The huge expanse of the sky and smell of the ocean, the people in real clothes who walked without restraint - the raw, beautiful freedom of it - made Mercie's eyes well with tears. She swallowed hard and made herself focus on the girl in front of her. The bold black 'ADC' on the back of the orange uniform was the ugliest thing she had ever seen.

The courtroom was cold and empty. The girls shuffled in from a hallway, directed to the jurors' box and commanded to keep their mouths shut. The double doors at the front hissed open. Several men and women in suits and way too much cologne walked in carrying briefcases and heavy folders. They exchanged pleasantries, holding the gate for each other, split up and took seats at the tables. Behind them the benches filled as more people entered. Some sat and stared daggers at the girls in chains.

Every time the doors hissed open everyone except the attorneys looked. Mercie glanced over and saw a kid stick his head in, looking right at her. She nearly wet herself.

The boy!

Taking a sharp breath, she wanted to stand and…
Do what, dummy?

The girl next to her said, "Don't let them see you cry, honey. Stay strong. Save the tears for the jury." She tried to pat Mercie's leg, cuffs and chain allowing a finger to brush it.

Mercie nodded and kept looking at the boy. His black hair was longer, in his eyes. He gave an awkward wave and tried to tell her something, but noticed everyone staring. He grinned at the room. Everyone turned back to the front.

She had never experienced such emotional turmoil. She was still trying to recover from seeing the outside world after weeks in isolation. And now here was the kid she assumed would be a witness against her, assumed he was back at home with his family, going to school and retelling the story of being kidnapped by a crazed bank robber… seeing his face made her relive it all in a moment. Throat tight, she couldn't swallow the memory of her dead parents.

She watched him through a blur, vision clearing as a realization struck. She hadn't been charged with kidnapping. No one even mentioned the boy being in the car, not the police or the newspapers. She had it in her mind they knew everything, that the bank's cameras had recorded it all and the boy would cooperate to hide the fact he was boosting stereos.

But the look on the boy's face told her she was wrong.

Did I pass out after we crashed?

His head vanished, door clicking shut. She blinked and sat up in her seat, questioning her sanity.

To the left of the judge's bench a man in a black robe walked through a door held by a deputy that looked well past retirement age. "All rise," the deputy said, looking around as if hoping someone would remain seated. "The Honorable Judge William D. Lee presiding. Take your seats."

Mercie sat and stared at her chains. The pulse in her wrists thudded against the cuffs. She looked up when the judge said something about who was first. He had the most annoying expression, high and mighty, ignoring the peasant prisoners while looking down his long nose at the lesser officers of the court. She knew it was all a show. A performance. In college she knew law students who talked about studying to be trial lawyers as if talking about learning to be actors. The fake, pretentious drama deciding the fate of millions made her sick. So the law students only included her in discussions about environmental law after that.

She smiled to herself. *Or debates about the food industry.*

Her mind wandered, blocking out the judge and attorneys taking turns speaking, the people in the audience looking on with the interest of movie buffs at an IMAX theater. She welcomed the distraction but lost the calming effect when she became aware of it.

She noticed her fists were clenched, red, and couldn't relax them. They rotated slightly with her pulse.

Sweat from her scalp cooled on her forehead. She dipped her head, attempting to wipe it on her shoulder. Looked at her lap and tried to stretch a finger to her face. The effort only made her look ridiculous and sweat even more. She had no clue how to wipe her face. Eyes burning, drops rolled off the end of her nose, onto her hands. The room became obscured in a bank of fog. She shivered.

The finger brushed her leg again. "Be strong," the girl whispered.

Nodding, she blinked her eyes clear and noticed the judge and attorneys were talking about her, looking over.

"Miss Hillbrook," the judge said. He looked at a woman sitting behind the prosecutors, the entire room following his eyes. She was scribbling furiously on a legal pad. His eyes moved back to Mercie. "Do you realize how much trouble you're in, young lady?"

***

"Damn, girl. You really do all that?" The girl behind Mercie whispered. They hobbled into a hallway in two lines, heading out of the building. "Motherfuckin' po-lice kill *my* folks, bank take *my* folks' shit, I wouldn't rob 'em - I'd shoot some big-ass holes in them niggas."

"Quiet up there!" the deputy walking behind them yelled.

Eleven pairs of shower shoes scuffed the linoleum, faint tinkles of chains brushing over thick uniforms. Mercie watched the feet of the girl in front of her, trying not to step on her heels. She couldn't wait to get out of there. She had lived a lifetime of constant embarrassment. Those varied incidents had nothing on the pure mortification experienced in that courtroom.

When the prosecutor read her charges and made his argument for an astronomical bond, she watched several reporters in the audience become very busy. The stares of the other prisoners bored into her. The judge scheduled a preliminary hearing three months from that day, to prepare for trial. She didn't want to think about coming back and going through that again.

The exit door popped open and the roar of freedom made her stumble. The deputy holding the door, usually one to sour-face women in chains, dropped her eyes when Mercie passed.

She stepped into sunshine and breathed relief. Then saw the cameras.

"Miss Hillbrook! Why did you do it?"

"Was it because police officers killed your parents?"

"Will you plead not guilty?"

"Mercie! Do you believe your parents were murdered by those police officers?"

Reporters fired questions walking on both sides of her. Men with cameras on their shoulders paced close behind them. Deputies flanked the lines and pushed between her and the reporters, yelling for them to move faster.

Mercie squinted ahead. The transport van, a filthy carrier of ruined lives, looked as inviting as *Chuck E. Cheese's*. Her chains rattled louder.

Next to the van's side doors stood a huge man in a local news tee shirt. He shouldered a camera and aimed it at the prisoners. They got closer and Mercie saw someone standing behind him.

Hiding behind him… She bit her lip.

A deputy stopped on the other side of the van doors and helped the girls in. Mercie shuffled up, next in line, and nearly jumped when a tawny little arm stuck out from next to the cameraman's thigh and forced a wad of paper into her hands. The arm disappeared just as fast. The deputy grabbed her and she gasped, turning frightened eyes on him, almost throwing the wad. She thought to eat it, but remembered she couldn't even wipe her face.

"Well, get in," the deputy said, angry. "Save that bullshit for another time. If you want to be a TV star, we aren't going to help you do it."

He helped her up the step, she ducked in and fell into a seat. Outside, the girl in line behind her turned to the camera and snapped, "Po-lice killed that girl's folks. Bank they say she robbed took her house. She ain't got nothing for collateral. That old mean-ass judge gave her a quarter-million dollar bond! Needs his old ass beat."

"Get in the van!"

The girl was grabbed and thrown in. She squealed with laughter. The others joined her, turning to tell Mercie the judge was wrong, she didn't deserve to be in jail. The side doors slammed, followed by the front. Traffic prevented the driver from venting his frustration on the engine and tires.

Bars on the side window cast shadows across Mercie's uniform. When the others lost interest in her she unfolded the wad of paper. Something shiny popped out. She barely caught it between two fingers. They shook as the shadows moved and revealed a handcuff key.

She cupped her other hand over it. As she jerked her eyes left, right, the collar of her shirt brushed over the base of her throbbing neck. The van went over potholes and turned, she swayed into the girl by the window. Their eyes met briefly. The girl looked at Mercie's hands, then went back to watching the cars, the businesses lining the highway.

Mercie unfolded the paper without looking at it, trying to watch everyone at once. Links on her chains shook, bloodless fingers clamped on the note. She moved it from between her legs, into a ray of light, and saw it was a used Burger King napkin. Written over ketchup stains was a message in block letters.

JUMP FINSE AND RUN ON TRANE TRACKS TO YAMOHA MOTOCYCEL SHOP. MEAT ME AT CAR. IT IS BLUE.

She balled it up, eyes darting. *Jump the fence? Run down the railroad tracks?* She looked at her stomach. *I can't jump a mud puddle.*

"Kid is nuts," she breathed.

She rolled her wrists and squinted at the key slots in the cuffs. She imagined herself taking off the chains, jumping out of the van… and falling on her face.

"Kid is *nuts.*"

The van turned onto the narrow lane leading to the jail, went through the gate and parked in the sally port. The girls were helped out. They lined up at the entry.

Mercie held the key and note tight. She stepped out of the van and tensed when a deputy grabbed her, helped her down. She stared at the thick steel entry door grinding open on its track. Beaded on her face, sweat trickled from tuffs of hair sticking to her cheeks. Slow, even breaths allowed her to walk without tripping on her shackles. Her hand throbbed around the key digging into her palm. She took a breath that relaxed her body but squeezed the key harder.

A girl by the door, taller and darker than the others, stood at the front of the line watching everyone get out. "Oh, uh-uh. That bitch *didn't do that,*" she said. She looked along the line of girls and jerked her head in Mercie's direction. "You see that bitch talking to them police?"

Mercie froze. She had been focused on the ground in front of her, the shackles snatching at her ankles, preventing full steps. Standing up straight, she became aware of a low voice - a deputy - asking questions, responses whispered to him. She couldn't hear what they were saying. The looks from the other girls made her stomach burn, her legs weaken.

Panic drove a cold wedge into the center of her chest. She heaved for breath and felt her guts roil and contract. Stopping, she closed her eyes and strained to hear. She recalled the girl sitting next to her, who pretended she hadn't seen Mercie hiding a waded napkin.

She looked at the girls and made her shower shoes. She shuffled towards them, wanting to ask them for help. The girl at the front of the line directed a look full of wicked rage at the snitch, hobbling to the rear of the line. "Whatever you got they gonna get it." She maintained her glower, a deputy grabbed her arm and escorted the line inside.

Mercie made it to the entry. The door grinded shut in her face. She faced the door, the light above it casting long shadows from the deputies walking up on both sides.

"Hillbrook! Step to the wall. Turn and put your nose on it."

The fear of being caught had slowly incapacitated her. Mind racing, she realized she didn't fear being caught anymore... and marveled at how quickly the spread of emotion turned her livid.

***

The lockdown cellblock was frigid. A thin green mattress, black wool blanket, and one set of clothes were the only allowable items. No TV, no magazines, no books, and even the mail was taken once it was read. Mercie sat on the bottom bunk, thankful another person wasn't in the cell. A blanket was wrapped around her shoulders, her bloodshot, emotionally voided stare worried a nurse that went cell-to-cell handing out prescription meds and offering Tylenol.

"Are you okay?" the nurse asked.

Mercie ignored her and stared at the floor. The deputy escorting the nurse looked in and said, "She's fine." The window brightened as they moved away.

A boiler room next to her cell made the concrete walls hum, a low droning that fluctuated in pitch. It never stopped. Random shouts and singing from the other cells seemed to add melody to the drone. Mercie liked the noise. It was tranquil. Despite recent events and the sleep deprivation - or maybe because of it - for the first time in weeks she could carefully pick through her thoughts.

They think someone put the handcuff key in the jury box...

A deputy told her she couldn't be charged with escape. But said she would be issued a Rules Violation Report for planning to escape. The RVR would be on her DOC record. Mercie didn't know what that meant. She did know it wouldn't matter once she was convicted of armed robbery.

She wanted it to be over. She didn't want a trial. She didn't want to be sentenced and left alone - she would trade whatever she might gain from a trial for that. Her life had been full of uncertainties before her parents had been killed. But never in her life did she imagine it would be this bad.

Leaning forward, elbows on knees, she cupped her face and rubbed her eyes. They were dry and sore. She looked at the sink, moving tongue over dry lips, but wasn't thirsty enough to brave drinking from the corroded tap. *Did dinner come already? Did I miss it?*

She blinked and looked around at the walls. She laughed at herself. "I was actually looking for a clock... *ha.*"

Outside her cell, on the far side of the dayroom, the entry slid open. Mercie heard yelling in the hallway, keys and boots busy around whoever was fighting. She stood at her door looking through the steel grate window. Two deputies rammed into the entry, shoulders hitting the frame hard. They maneuvered in, dragging a girl in orange by her arms. The girl screamed and kicked at more deputies attempting to grab her feet. Blood poured from a deep gash on the side of her face. Mercie's breath caught as she recognized the tattle-tale.

A deputy opened a corner cell. The screaming prisoner was dragged in and handcuffed to the bunk. Threats and demands for a hospital followed the deputies out, muting as the heavy cell door slammed.

Mercie's eyes tracked drops of blood across the dayroom, from corner to entry. Juanita walked in, hands cuffed behind her. Long strands of dark hair stood up from her tight ponytail. Smears of blood painted her tee shirt. Two deputies followed her, one with a tight grip on her handcuffs. In no hurry, Juanita stopped and looked into a cell held open by a tall, angry deputy. Juanita squinted and walked over to the cell next to Mercie. She stopped and waited for it to be unlocked.

The deputy holding her handcuffs laughed. "Why not? For what you did to that snake you can have that privilege." She unlocked the cuffs. "Too bad you didn't kill her. Would've done everyone a favor." She closed the cell and looked at Mercie, smiling.

What the freaking Twilight Zone was that all about?

The tattle-tale continued to rant, kicking her bunk, long after the deputies left. Mercie bumped her fist on the wall and whispered out the window. "Juanita."

Juanita bumped the wall twice.

"Thank you..."

Juanita bumped once.

***

Mercie flinched and opened her eyes. The dream replayed as she remembered where she was: the deputies taking the note and key from her hands; the tattle-tale escorted past her; her nose pressed to the bricks, hands on her shoulders holding her there.

A new scene played out briefly: Juanita being told about Mercie getting caught, and how... taking a razor blade to the tattle-tale's face.

Mercie smiled and closed her eyes. The rolled up end of the mattress crinkled under her neck. It smelled, and the blanket wasn't long enough to cover her feet. She was beyond caring. Sleep took her again. Hours later she nearly hit her head on the top bunk, sitting up when the lock on her cell opened.

"You're free to go, Miss Hillbrook."

Her pulse thrummed at the words. She narrowed her eyes, unable to see the man's face. She recognized the voice, though.

"Perez?" She put on her shower shoes, stood with the blanket around her.

"Chief Perez, yes." He hitched up his pants. "I don't know how you did it, lady, but I'm here to tell you I

will find out. I will find that money. And if any of it was used to post this bail I will arrest the person aiding and abetting you." He didn't wait for a reply. Turned and swaggered to the exit.

She walked after him, wishing her eyes were lasers so she could burn him in half. They went to the front of the jail. A short black lady with glasses and big hair smiled at them, introduced herself to Mercie.

"Erica Reed, of Reed's Bail bonds." They shook hands. "You're famous again." She took a newspaper from a briefcase, handed it over.

Mercie held the paper, about to burst with questions. Something told her to contain herself. Nothing mattered except that she was about to walk out of there.

Chief Perez watched them closely. "Who posted the bail, Erica?"

Erica smiled at Mercie and talked to him like she would a kindergartner. "That's confidential, sweetheart."

"No, that's bullshit." He shouted for the control room to buzz the exit.

***

Erica steered her truck onto the highway, accelerated into the fast lane. "Where to?" She had an easy smile. "Normally I charge extra for cab services, but your friend put a nice tip in my tip jar, girl." She laughed and turned on some music.

Mercie, wearing the clothes she had been arrested in, sat in the passenger seat looking at the newspaper on her lap. The front page showed a photo of two police officers with the caption, "BACK ON THE JOB". She read the article quickly, then once more, memorizing the names.

Erica hummed a Mary J. Blige song. She said, "I'm sorry about your mom and dad. Don't let that," she nodded at the paper, "get to you, honey. That's just life. Learn from it, and gain strength from it." She alternated her attention between the road and her client.

Mercie looked up. "I'll be okay. Thanks…"

"Cried it all out? I see the way you're looking at those two cops. Whatever you're thinking, stop thinking it."

Mercie kept reading, tapping a finger on her lip.

"Well, while you're thinking… whatever. Think of a place I can drop you off. Much as I enjoy your company, I have a couple of teenagers I have to round up and force to do homework."

She folded the paper. "Sorry. Things have been so crazy. I haven't been myself. Thanks for the ride. I don't know why I didn't ask where we were going… or tell you where I need to go. Actually, I don't have anywhere to go." She looked out the window. Noticed her reflection and finger combed her hair.

"How about I take you where your friend is staying?"

Mercie's lips pursed. "How much did he pay you?"

She grinned, showing a flash of gold at the corner of her mouth. "That boy is a seasoned hustler. Your bond was two hundred and fifty thousand. Usually takes ten percent or less to post bail. Little man walked into my office, told me this big-ass lie, and put thirty grand on my desk like he was buying a Pepsi.

"I told him to get his little ass out of my business before I called the cops." She glanced over. "I wouldn't have, though. Before I could get him out, the joker talked me into the bail. He started over, told me everything. After hearing your story I got mad. And when I get mad I want to get even. Everyone knows about your mom and dad, even people that don't watch the news."

Picturing all that made her smile. "He tell you he was trying to steal my stereo?"

"Out of the car you stole, yeah." They laughed together.

Mercie felt grateful to the boy, and to this woman. She didn't know how to express it. Her parents were the only people to ever care about her, help her. And no one had ever done anything like this, risking their freedom, for her. A hand closed over hers.

"It's okay, honey. You don't have to say anything. I feel for you and your folks. But I did my part for the money. Ain't no sense in me pretending otherwise." Her laugh was loud. "We cool, though. I've been paid. You just focus on getting your business together."

"Thank you." The hand squeezed and let go.

She read the article again but her attention kept wandering. *I don't even know that kid's name... Does he live with his family? By himself... in a tree house, or something?*

Erica turned off the highway. Mercie's eyes went wide; they were heading toward her neighborhood in Gautier. The little brick houses and patches of woods, the kids playing in the street, were experienced from a new perspective.

She was no longer the daughter of Mister and Mistress Hillbrook; she had broken free of that shell of naiveté. She would miss her parents dearly, but would not miss her former self. She lost everything she came from, and would lose much of her future. But she had never felt more *alive* than at that moment. After the deaths, the crimes and degrading treatment of incarceration... there was nothing left to fear.

The orange glare of street lights illuminated the boughs of towering pines and ancient oaks lining the *cul de sac*. At the apex the house her attention was riveted to still looked the same, simple red bricks flanked by flower beds. She half expected her mom to come out and tell her leftovers were in the fridge.

The yard, though, had a minor change with drastic meaning: a realty sign.

Erica parked in front of the mailbox. Dug in her purse. "Remember what I said." She looked at the newspaper in Mercie's hands. "Call me if you forget. Accidentally or on purpose. Any time." She handed over a business card and grinned.

Mercie thanked her, closed the door and turned to study the sign, the roar of the truck fading behind her. She stepped in the tall grass, crickets scattering from her boots. Grabbing the sign, she yanked it straight up and slammed it down. Boot lifted, she paused at seeing the realtor's name: MacIntyre.

"No way…"

Opening the newspaper, she quickly scanned the front page. Under the photos a caption read, "Officers Jesse Sanchez and Craig MacIntyre back on duty."

That's insane. Has to be a coincidence…

Her next thought added to the insanity. "Page," she whispered, seeing the nameplate on the bank executive's desk. "Page Douche-canoe *MacIntyre*."

Crumpling the paper she raised a boot and stomped hard, growling. Her balance betrayed her, boot sliding on the new sign, and she ended up on her back with no breath and crickets jumping over her face.

She gasped, hand on chest, looking at black clouds floating by overhead, stars twinkling through. The garage door stuttered and slid open, making her turn and get a good whiff of wet dirt. She saw brand-new Nikes, too big for the owner, approach. She looked back at the clouds and the boy's face appeared above her's.

"Did you get it?" His crooked teeth showed in a confused smile.

She sighed. "No…"

His face disappeared, grass crunching next to her. She looked at her legs, past her boots. The boy jumped up and down on the sign, flailing his arms and shouting with each blow. He apparently forgot the seriousness of the task, laughing before he quit.

"There are more signs over there." He pointed to the next street over. His eyebrows raised. "Wanna go get those, too?"

She said, "No." Lines disappeared from her forehead, creasing her cheeks. "Yes. Help me up."

***

The last time she saw him he wore clothes that appeared to have been used to wipe grease off machines before he put them on. His crisp new jeans, bright yellow shirt and sneakers with the tags still on them made him look like a completely different kid. He took a huge smartphone from his back pocket and sat on the floor where her parents' couch used to be.

At the front of the living room near the windows she sat and leaned against the wall, studying him.

Glancing at the bare walls he said, "I wanted to get new pictures. And some," he gestured at the round depressions in the carpet, "furniture…"

"But?"

"I don't know where to get it."

"Is that right? Well, let's say you did know. What kind of pictures and furniture would you get?"

His mouth twisted. He tapped the phone on his leg and pointed at the wall separating the living room and kitchen. "I would put a big monster picture right there." His eyes moved to her, back to the wall. "With a black frame?"

"Was that a question? Thought you had it all figured out."

"I do." He straightened his back.

"Uh-huh. Ok, big monster in a black frame. What kind of furniture?" Stretching out her legs, she crossed her boots.

"Um." He looked at her boots, skirt, at her shoulders. "A big chair. And, um, a big couch."

She burst out laughing. "Are you saying I'm fat? Do I look like I need big furniture?"

"No…" His confused and crooked smile appeared. He looked at his scrawny arms and wrinkled his nose. Pinched his stomach. "How do I get big like you? I want to need big furniture, too."

"Nice save." She almost fell over giggling. "Oh, you're a riot, kid. Hand me your phone and I'll show you how to get big like me."

An hour later they were surrounded by delivery containers. Pizza, pasta, and cheesy bread permeated the house. With no cups they had to drink from bottles. Mercie gripped the neck of her Mr. Pibb two-liter and turned it up with one hand, chasing a huge bite of cheesy bread. It fizzled when she set it down.

She looked over at the boy. He had pizza sauce all over his mouth and hands, spots on his clothes. Every time he took a drink he tried to hold the bottle with one hand and couldn't prevent soda from escaping his lips. Rivulets spread over his neck, wetting the sauce spots on his shirt. He grinned and wiped his face on a sleeve.

She pointed at a stack of napkins. He looked around, slid a pizza box over and dropped his slice in.

Grabbed a few napkins. His face didn't look right with a serious expression. She bit her lip. With great care he dabbed at his mouth, getting none of the sauce off.

"Eat up," she murmured around a bite of pasta. "We don't have a refrigerator to keep leftovers in." She slurped more off her plastic fork.

He sighed, leaned back and looked at his swollen stomach. He frowned and rubbed it. "I've never eaten this much. Think I need to use the bathroom."

She stabbed at more pasta. "'This much'? Don't quit on me now. We still have dessert. Go make some more room." She pointed her fork at the hallway, smiling.

His eyes closed. He groaned and struggled to his feet. She barely held in a laugh, coughing instead, when he swayed and stumbled off to the bathroom.

She yelled after him, "Lightweight!"

***

It was still in the wastebasket liners. The three plastic bags were in the corner of her bedroom. Next to them was a pallet of blankets and a green sleeping bag that looked as if rats had chewed tunnels through it.

One of the bags was open. She squatted, grabbed it and looked in. The faces of Franklin, Grant and Jackson looked back at her. Her pulse quickened. Hands moving fast, she opened each bag and poured the money into a pile. Separating the bundles, she counted out $45,000. There were some loose bills, another grand or so.

"*Shit,*" she breathed.

She turned as the boy walked in. He looked a lot better, though still held his stomach. Her mind hummed with questions. She opened her mouth, closed it. Standing, she puffed out her cheeks, closed her eyes and shook her head. She gave a small laugh. "I'm Mercie."

He looked up. "I'm Kermit."

"Like the frog?"

"Yep. Like the big cool frog on TV."

"That your real name?" She put a hand on her hip.

"Cong is my real name. But it's a stupid name."

"What's wrong with it? I actually like it. Mercie is a stupid name." She thumbed the loose bills.

He shrugged. "When I was in school some guys made fun of me. They said I had a weird name. They said I looked weird, too." He dropped his eyes. "I got into fights all the time."

"And they kicked you out. I understand. Believe me, I understand." She smacked him on top of the head with the money. "You got into fights because you had the courage to fight back. Every single day I wish I had the courage to fight the people that hurt me." She smacked him again and he smiled.

"I'll help you fight them." He swung a few punches, his expression harsh.

She looked at the bundles of money. "You already have, Kermit."

***

"I'm surprised the power isn't off."

"I turned it back on."

"Isn't that…" She was going to say 'illegal'. She gave a rueful chuckle. "How did you manage that?"

Kermit tilted his head, dark eyes looking up through locks of black hair. Mouth turned up at a corner. "I watched the power man put plastic," he gestured with his hands, "things on the meter. I took them off when he left."

"Why?" A soft luster shown from Mercie's eyes.

She wanted to goad him into revealing his criminal life, but didn't want to offend him.

He shrugged, held up his phone. "Had to charge."

"Let me see that."

They sat on her bedroom floor, the bundles of cash between them. The complete silence of the house seemed to make the bare walls desolate. He took a drink from his two-liter, carbonated fizz popping when he set it between his legs. As he watched her tap away on the touch screen he fidgeted, wanting her to show him what she was doing.

Noticing his burning curiosity she smiled, crossed her legs and held the phone closer to her face. Without looking at him she said, "You have clothes here? Food?" She looked over the top of the phone. "How in the world did you know I lived here, anyway?"

He pointed at the phone, nodded at the window. "The news people were in front of your house. They said your parents were killed by police officers. So you robbed a bank, or something. The news vids were on Facebook."

The mischievous glitter returned to her eyes. "Are you even old enough to be on Facebook?"

Scowling, he sat up tall. "I'm eighteen."

"Uh-huh. Minus five."

He kept scowling, took another drink of soda. She pursed her lips, fighting a giggle.

Holding up the phone again she logged into her Wells Fargo account and ordered a new debit card. All her possessions were in her bedroom when the bank repossessed the house. Her wallet had been in the compartment under the seat of her scooter, a fact she remembered later that night in a freezing cell. The bank would 'over-night' a new card by FedEx. They would need it to order new clothes online.

She pinched the hem of her skirt. *Ugh. I'm not going in public until I get new clothes and a shower… and a car.*

"Craigslist," she muttered.

"I like Craigslist," He was smiling again.

"What do you know about Craigslist?"

His eyebrows pushed together. "I sell stereos on there." He held his hands apart. "And speakers."

"Of course you do." The battery was nearly dead. She handed the phone to him. "We'll need a full charge for tomorrow. Get some sleep, bud."

***

The owner wouldn't drive the six miles to their house. They had to walk to his.

What an ass-hat. She pushed a lock of hair out of her eyes. A strong breeze scattered leaves over the street, her boots crushing them. *What a douche-canoe…*

Kermit showed no signs of embarrassment; his shirt billowed in the sunshine, the bright yellow glowing around the sauce and soda stains. His crooked, carefree smile shown just as bright and stained.

Mercie, however, felt her embarrassment grow with each passing car. If she hadn't experienced the degradation at the jail she wouldn't have even left the house. Her hair, shirt, and the back of her skirt were drenched with sweat. She kept checking Google Maps on Kermit's phone, boots kicking up pebbles at the base of driveways.

"Are we really getting a Challenger?" He ran forward and punted a beer can. It caught air, smacked into a mailbox.

"If it looks good and drives good, like the ad promised." A huge trickle of sweat traced her spine, into her underwear. She grumbled in thought, *It* better *look good and drive good... stupid douche-canoe dude.*

"Is that it? Is that the car? Are we gonna get it?" Excited, he skipped and pointed ahead to the right.

The street curved, went straight again. She looked at the phone, squinted at the other side of the curve. They passed under a tree, limbs casting dappled shadows, and she suddenly saw the car. The Dodge Challenger was parked at the foot of a driveway, passenger tires in the gutter. The tinted windshield had $15,000 painted across the top in white, blinding reflection of the sun below it making the bright yellow paint job look white.

She stopped walking. Her feet ached. Her lower back was on fire. The sweat between her thighs and in her armpits made her feel like a Neanderthal. Seeing the car, a little fantasy played in her mind - her behind the wheel, laughing wildly, screaming V8 and long black marks - made all the discomfort vanish.

"Yes," she said, walking again. She reached under her shirt, pulled a bundle of cash from her waist. "We're gonna get it."

He whooped and sprinted around. Skipped alongside her again. "I like the color."

"It has a Hemi."

"Alright!" He whooped and skipped around her once more. "What's a Hemi?"

"I have no idea." She pressed her lips together as if savoring something delicious. "But it's really cool."

***

She didn't need a test drive. She sat in the driver's seat and felt an immediate effect of the black leather hugging her: her confidence was restored.

Papers signed, the seller walked up his driveway with a big grin. She watched him talk to his wife who stood in the open garage. Starting her new machine, she noticed the fuel tank was full. "Maybe he isn't a douche-canoe. But he's still an ass-hat."

"Ass-hat!" Kermit's laugh was suddenly cut off, his head sticking to the seat. Mercie raced them out of the neighborhood, tires chirping at every intersection.

She took the remaining bills from her waist, dug her bank card from the middle of them and handed it to Kermit. "You know how to use that?"

"I've had a bunch of these. Um…"

"That didn't belong to you. Just say, 'No, I don't know how to use it'."

He looked at the back of the card, glanced at her like she made him eat a whole plate of brussel sprouts. "I don't know how."

They came up on a truck going too slow. She checked the mirrors, passed it, grinning because the tires barked when it downshifted.

"Wells Fargo." He examined his phone as if he could swipe it there.

"We need clothes. You can shop for your own."

"Shop, like, at Wal-Mart dot com?"

"Yes. No." She gave him a look. "We can afford better. Try Kohl's."

"Why can't I just use the money? We can go to the store."

"You can. And we will. But you need to learn how to use a debit card. You can't go around spending a lot of cash."

"Why?" He studied the magnetic strip, tongue poking out.

She thought about the money they stashed in the

attic. A stab of fear pricked her guts, and she wasn't sure why. "It's safer. I think. I can't explain why. I just know we can't spend the cash all the time. We can use my savings since, well, I don't have any bills. I mean, we get free power now."

He tapped the card on his knee. "Think I saw something like that on TV. The cops busted these bank robbers because they kept buying things."

The prick of fear intensified. She looked at the Dodge emblem on the steering wheel and winced. "Yeah… That was pretty stupid of them, huh?"

"It kinda was. They were buying fancy cars and clothes, gold chains," he touched his neck, "stuff like that. One guy bought a condo with a waterfall. It was tight." He nodded. "But they were really dumb robbers."

"Well…" She looked at the hood and sighed. *Had to get bright freaking yellow, didn't I?* "We should try to avoid doing what they did. We're used to not having much, anyway."

"Mmm-hmm." He set the card and phone in his lap, turned to her. "Do you miss your mom and dad?"

"Yes. Of course. But I try not to think about it."

He chewed on his lip. "Because it hurts?"

She didn't answer, lost in thought. She was actually glad the house was barren. If she had to see her dad's chair, coffee cup and reading glasses, her mom's bookshelf and plants hanging in the kitchen… their framed portraits in the hallway…

The road blurred. She cleared her throat. "Because it hurts."

He looked up, held out a hand to catch himself on the dashboard, car abruptly slowing. Mercie did a U-turn, big engine growling. She growled with it, overcorrecting as they slid sideways. They zoomed through traffic. Kermit saw her expression change and sat up to see ahead, looking for police. "Where are we going?"

She snarled, grip tightening on the wheel.

"Ok." He put on his seatbelt.

The bank had opened moments ago, only a few cars in the parking lot. Mercie turned in, front-end dipping on the slight incline, tires barking as she stomped the brake, sliding into a slot. The Challenger rumbled at idle, quieted. She debated taking out the key. Left it in, listening to the Hemi tick. Staring at the gauges behind the wheel she felt Kermit's eyes on her.

"This isn't Kohl's." He turned and looked at the bank. "This is a bad idea." Stuffing the phone and card in his pockets, head turning to check all directions, he put a hand on the door latch.

She looked at him. "I'll be right back. Stay in the car." She opened the door. Horizontal rays from the morning sun made her pale face shine. She moved her face into the shadow of a light pole, studying the front of the bank.

"What if you need my help?" He got out.

"I won't. I'm just going in to talk."

"You bring a gun?" He looked at her skirt.

"What? No. I said *talk*, not rob. Don't worry."

"Why are you so angry? Are you mad at me for asking about your mom and dad?" He followed her to the lobby door.

She snatched open the door. A blast of air chilled her sweaty hair, penetrating through the heat of rage.

What the hell am I doing?

The door hissed shut behind her. A teller looked up, saw Mercie and screamed. The other tellers looked and added their own exclamations. A door behind them opened. Mercie saw the bank executive and flushed, chill evaporating.

"Page. *MacIntyre.*" Her ominous tone rolled over the silent lobby.

Page froze. Hand still on her office door, she looked in, turned her confused gaze on the tellers. Her head jerked back to Mercie, hands pressed to her chest.

The teller closest to Page, a slim brunette in a navy blue pantsuit, shouted at her boss. "Tell her to leave! She can't be in here!" Fear strained her voice as she turned to Mercie. "Didn't the court tell you, you couldn't come in here?"

Skinny bitch... money slut... Mercie cast a baleful look in her direction. She blinked and shut out everything but Page.

A tug on her arm became a dragging weight, and she realized Kermit was scraping across the carpet. He held onto her wrist with both hands. She shook him off and ran to catch the office door before Page could lock herself in. She lunged and Page smashed Mercie's boot in between the door and frame, a terrorized shriek sounding in the gap.

Mercie pushed into the room easily. Closed the door and leaned against it. "Hello again."

"Miss Hillbrook. What an unexpected... visit." She gulped a breath. "What-what are you doing here?" Backing around her desk, she grabbed her chair and wheeled it in front of her.

Mercie stabbed a finger at the nameplate on the desk. "MacIntyre. What can MacIntyre do for me? How about what has MacIntyre *done* to me? Let's see." She held up a hand. Baring her teeth behind it, she counted off on her fingers. "Murdered my parents. Stole everything they had worked for their entire lives." Her voice broke. "Wrecked my entire world, you cockroach!" She pushed off the door and stalked to the desk, put her fists on it. "You took my family. You or whoever you work for took their *lives!* I can't prove it right now. But I will."

"Those are false accusations. Threats! The police are on the way. You are a criminal. You robbed this bank! I'll have you arrested for coming in here like this and slandering my reputation." Her lower eyelids climbed up her wide eyeballs, lips quivering. Her fingers dug into the back of the chair. *"Get out of my bank!"*

"I hear sirens. Come on!" Kermit yelled from the lobby.

Mercie punched the desk. It took all her will to keep from screaming in pain, hand instantly going numb. She turned and opened the office door. The tellers stared at her. She spun and shouted a curse at Page that came out as a spitting growl, looked down and swatted an ivy plant from a table and ran out of the bank, maniacal grin stretching her face.

***

Page heard a car race away out front and sighed, her entire body sagged. She glanced out at the tellers, walked over and slammed her office door. Behind her desk she plopped in her chair, opened a side drawer and took out her handbag. Dug out a bottle of Loratabs. Ate two, dry. Replacing the bottle she took out a cell phone and dialed a number.

"She knows," she told the person that answered. "I don't know how. Just take care of it. I have to go."

Replacing the phone and bag in the drawer, she locked it and stood, gathering her thoughts on what to tell the police.

Nothing, she decided. *Nothing happened…*

***

"Ha ha. I got him again."

"Kermit! I'm no expert, but I'm pretty sure that was me you just got again."

"Oh. Are we on the same team?"

"Yeah. So get the other guys with guns."

"Okay. They should have let you be a girl."

"They should have."

An explosion lit up the room. The moans of the burning, dying enemy made Kermit smile. The screen of the huge smart TV changed. Rock music blared in time with strobes of yellow-gold on their intent faces, followed by a new score chiming.

Mercie squirmed on her beanbag, looking closely at her PS4 controller. "How did you do that?"

"Look out!" He held up his controller as if to block a blow, thumbs tapping hard on the buttons. The room bloomed with light again, the explosion - in surround sound - vibrating the bare walls. "Never mind," he sighed. "You're dead again."

"Dude! Quit that!"

He leaned over and grabbed a two-liter bottle of Barq's, drank deeply, facing the TV. His eyes turned toward her.

"Yeah, I suck." She stuck out her tongue.

She rocked back and forth, her controller plopped on the carpet as she stood, beanbag creaking. Groaning, she pressed her hands to her lower back and stretched. Looking over at Kermit she lifted a boot and feigned a kick, giggling when he shouted and fell over.

Hand on the tight waist of her new pants, she admired the way her turquoise shirt looked with the video game flickering over it. *Nice... but I think I was feeling overly optimistic when I bought these pants.*

"Are there any more tacos?"

She rubbed her waist and grinned. "Yep."

"The rolled ones?"

"You ate all of those. We have hard or soft. Choose your poison, bud." She walked into the kitchen.

"Hard!" He frowned, tongue moving over the roof of his mouth. "Soft!"

She laughed. "Okay."

Stepping to the counter she looked in the Taco Bell bags, grabbed one and re-joined him in the living room. "You lightweight little - " She stopped and held her breath, fanning away a plume of smoke. Threw the bag in Kermit's lap, moved to stand in front of him.

He looked up at her glare. "Hey! I almost burned myself." He moved the bag to the floor, put a broken cigarette to his lips and lit it. Smoke rushed out of his nostrils. "Check out my lighter." He held up a small butane torch and clicked it on. The thrusting flame made a blue shadow across his eyes. "Cool, huh?"

"No. It's a stupid lighter."

"Huh?" Confusion and hurt strained his expression when he realized she was looking at him in disgust.

"You're smoking. So that makes the lighter stupid. It was used for a stupid thing." She folded her arms. "Everything about smoking is stupid. It makes those awesome new jeans stupid. Your new phone and Nikes?" Her eyebrows lifted. "Stupid. Doesn't matter how cool your lighter or anything is. The coolest looking dude in the world looks stupid the moment he puts a cigarette in his mouth."

"Oh." He dropped the Camel in his Barq's and watched it float, minuscule bubbles popping around it.

"Touching lesson."

Mercie shouted and spun around, kermit scrambling to his feet next to her. Two men stood in the dining room. The door to the garage was open behind them. They were dressed in black, ski masks covering faces. The guns they held riveted her attention and she noticed nothing else.

"Effective lesson." The man on the left waggled his gun like it was a wine glass. "Telling kids they'll get cancer never works."

Handing his gun to his partner the man who spoke opened a cargo pocket on his pants, took out a roll of duct tape. "Both of you put your hands behind your head. And don't move. Don't even talk. Nod if you understand."

A powerful hand grabbed Mercie's wrists one at a time, held them together. A strip of wide, pinching tape compressed her wrists, twisted muscles in her shoulders. She gritted her teeth and nodded.

He taped Kermit's wrists the same way, heavy breaths puffing out of his ski mask, jerking the boy back and forth. Mercie sensed his sneer and knew a plea for Kermit's life would only fuel their cruelty.

They were turned around. The partner held a gun on each of them. His masked head looked too small for his body. He said, "You don't want to do it here? I think we can do it here."

"No. We'll take them to the marsh." His gloved hands clamped down on their upper arms, pushed them apart. Standing between them he leaned over and told Kermit in a gentle tone, "It's gonna be okay, boy. Now quit your crying or else I'm gonna have to hurt your friend here." Kermit's shuddering chest froze. He looked up and the man nodded. He said in that same pacifying voice, "I will smash her teeth in with my boot and make you watch.

We don't want that now, do we? Good."

"Tape their mouths. Then they can't cry out."

"No shit. Just keep an eye on the street. I'm just fucking with the boy."

Lengths of tape were strapped tightly over their lips. Mercie's cheeks pulled together and she had to squint hard to keep her eyes focused. She glanced at her friend and bit back a sob; tears were already pouring over the tape on his mouth.

He's going to be killed because of me...

These were the officers, the murderers, she knew. She didn't need to see their faces, didn't need a P.I. license to figure out the *why?* of the situation. These two men shot her parents for money. And they would shoot her and anyone else to keep that from being known.

The cold reality was sinking in, trepidation buzzing her into a state of sickening paralysis. Her energy, vibrant and optimistic as they played video games and chowed down pizza, vanished with the freedom to move her arms or speak. Fighting nausea, she swayed, moaned, staring at the gun pointed at her face hoping it would somehow keep her from fainting...

Had to go to the bank, didn't you?

Eyes reeling back into darkness, she heard the voice of her mother. *Mom?*

Never consider what you're about to say. You just shoot off at the mouth, with your big words and fancy college degree.

Her temples throbbed, eyes writhing in their sockets. *Mom! What should I do?*

A familiar tisking cut through the vertigo. *Mercie Elene, how many times must I tell you? A man has his muscles; a woman has her mind.*

"What's wrong with her?"

"She's gonna pass out. Let's fucking go. Look at

her. If she falls out we won't be able to carry her fat ass. We can't be seen putting her in the Denali."

"You two getting high?" The man with the tape looked around at the beanbags, the fast-food and shipping packages full of clothes. "Alcohol?"

"Who gives a fuck if they're high? We're not exactly law officers right now. Go get the wheels. Just drive around to the kitchen patio. We don't have time to move that piece of shit in the garage."

"Okay, alright." He pocketed the tape. Went into the garage and shut the door behind him.

Mercie had recovered enough that she could stand straight and see clearly. But it was hard to think with her heart hammering and Kermit wheezing through his snot filled nose; his trouble breathing exacerbated his panic, and hers. They didn't have long, only minutes. She knew if they were driven away from here they were dead.

The man chewed on something, holes in his ski mask elongating. His relaxed hands held the guns at waist height, aimed at their torsos. She blinked and dropped her head, keeping up the sick act, looking at the man closely for the first time. The slackness in her face tightened, and she stopped her expression from changing suddenly. Between his boots was an impression in the carpet. An old one, from her dad's chair. The flattened circle of carpet made her remember the man who used to sit there. Made her remember the comfort he gave her with only his presence. She felt that part of her missing, an inflamed crevice she slipped into, like a heavy coat.

"Mmnnagh," she groaned against the tape. Hands clamped onto her shoulder, fingers pressing deep.

"Well, fucking help me with this fat bitch," Jesse said. His gun slid from his waist onto her breasts. A curse spit on the inside of his ski mask. He grabbed the gun, passed it back to Craig.

Taking the gun Craig said, "I'm doing what you told me to do. *Your* plan. I tell you again, it's too risky bringing them to the marsh." His masked head turned slowly towards Kermit and tilted slightly. The twin Sig Sauers shifted in his fists. "Come on, Jesse," he whined. "Here. *Now.* I'll do them both with a knife. We'll make it look like a robbery and we can take the fancy TV." Still looking at Kermit his head tilted a little more when the boy's breathing became short gasps. His tiny throat pulsed in and out, heaving for air that bubbled deep in his sinuses. Mucus streamed out of his nose, over the tape. His eyes, swollen with strain, pumped tears in sync with his gasps.

Craig rubbed the gun in his right hand against the front of his pants. "Maybe it'll be a case of rape and murder, open and closed."

Jesse let Mercie drop back on the floor. "I knew it. That's why you want to ice them here."

Craig held the guns above his shoulders, pointed at the ceiling. "Whoa, let's not get the ethics board involved here. You'll get no awards for taking them to that creature in the marsh, either."

"Yeah, but he doesn't rape them."

"No. He only feeds them to giant alligators. And you don't know what he does to them before that."

"He kills them clean and disposes of the remains." He pointed at Kermit. "He doesn't torture little boys and fuck them."

Craig sighed, dropped the guns to his sides and grumbled, "You don't know that…"

Jesse clenched his gloved fists, stepped over Mercie. "I'm going to get the Denali. You stay here." He took his gun back and pointed it at his partner's crotch. "No fucking around, understand?"

Mercie peeked to see Craig's jaw working back and forth under the mask, watching Jesse leave, boots echoing through the garage. Gun held rigid at his side, Craig's neck bulged with a growling whine. His petulant act in response to being denied the pleasure of raping Kermit unnerved her. She couldn't believe this man was an actual police officer.

Her hyper-extended shoulders felt as if dislocation was imminent and would be memorable. But the fiery tears stretching from her joints, up her neck, down her spine, were the only reason she hadn't reacted to the terror her friend was experiencing. She had to stall for more time.

Why? There's no escaping this…

She couldn't feel the tape strapped to her wrists any longer. The searing burn flowed past her elbows and deadened. Her focus held there, blocking out everything else. Ignoring the strong instinct to struggle, scream for help, for their deaths. Ignoring her instinct to *fight for her life.*

She peeked again. Craig was still staring at Kermit. He shrugged and said, "Why not? We killed her parents." His head tilted in her direction. "Took everything they had. We'll get a nice paycheck from this house. What difference could it possibly make if we take our pleasure with you, too?" He stopped rubbing himself and laughed.

She couldn't help squeezing her eyes tightly shut and silently cursed. Letting her face go slack on the carpet, she made her eyelids flutter, showing whites.

The county jail had been an almost daily stage for such acts. She had witnessed several girls' fake injuries, seizures, even a heart attack. She hoped her act was as convincing as theirs. With her mouth taped she feared flopping around with a full-on 'seizure'. The result would likely be a more painful death than whatever the Marsh Creature will do: death by Taco Bell vomit.

Her head bobbed off the floor with a convulsive swallow.

Which may happen anyway, lying perfectly still...

Craig's demeanor changed as the large SUV rumbled by the side of the house, parked by the kitchen door. "Finally," He said and scratched at his neck with the barrel of the gun.

A gust of wind slammed the screen door behind Jesse. Mercie flinched. Jesse's boots pounded over the tile, onto the living room carpet. Her pulse thundered in her ears, temples.

What do I do now?

She had merely stalled the inevitable. These men were professional killers. There was no chance she could stop them or help Kermit get away. There was no one coming to their rescue. Playing dead and hoping for a miracle escape strategy was a grasp at old pine straw, soggy cellulose that couldn't save an arachnid from drowning.

Hands dug into her sides. Then she *did* struggle. She did scream for help, for their deaths. She did fight for her life...

A spike of regret pressed her tongue to the roof of her mouth a second before the butt of the gun cracked against her skull.

"She's not faking now." Craig looked at the blood on his gun and chuckled. "Page said that fat bitch was crazy."

Jesse ignored him, relieved the belligerent girl was out cold. They each grabbed an arm and dragged her across the floor.

The tape over Kermit's mouth puffed out with a high pitched keening. He sank to the floor, hyperventilating.

***

"Well, well." Her mom's voice drifted into her shell of darkness. *'Was that too tough for Miss Know It All? Giving up already? I thought you wanted to be somebody. You'll be lucky to serve fries and burgers.'*

Mercie could hear the smile at the end, could almost see the manicured hand on her hip, stern, regal eyes boring into hers as she made Mercie aware of her need for humility.

"But, *Mom…*"

In the thick ether blackness, a soft glow bloomed, flesh toned swirls like a scattering of migratory birds suddenly emerged into a flock, forming a woman's head. A silhouette of thick curls framed high cheekbones, a reproachful finger wagged in front of large glasses with clear loving eyes that seemed to know her every thought before she did.

"Don't 'But Mom' me, young lady." The finger ticked side to side, and Mercie felt herself shrink until she had to look straight up at her impossibly tall, disgruntled mother.

Gigantic Mom put a manicured hand behind her head and pushed up at the bottom of her curls. Her countenance allowed the smile to form fully now that her daughter had submitted her want to argue.

Mercie sobbed, hit by a wave of emotion pulsing across the eerie dream well, bathing her in unfiltered, motherly compassion. The feeling was as familiar as her mother's hugs, the laughs she shared with her father at the dinner table…

The blackness returned in total, and with it the reality of loss. Her parents would never be around to give her advice again.

But their memories would.

Mom had a point. Her mom's admonishments were never harsh lectures that sought to control her. They were struck, brief, said in a way to teach so that Mercie realized the lesson on her own.

"Was that too tough for Miss Know It All? Giving up already? I thought you wanted to be somebody. You'll be lucky to serve fries and burgers."

Her eyes flared open. A snarl burbled against the tape. She exhaled hard through her nose to clear it and rolled her face away from the belt buckle creasing her cheek. Looked down the length of her legs. Duct tape was wrapped tightly around her boots. Her eyebrows pinched together. *Shit!*

The fresh resolve inspired by Mom faltered when the engine started. The front doors slammed. Her numb arms were useless though, they kept her from rolling onto the floorboard, the Denali reversing quickly to the street.

Mom? At this point I'll be fortunate to ever serve fries and burgers. What else you got?

The heavy SUV rolled off the soft grass onto the pavement. Swayed, shifting into drive. Two gunshots boomed like explosions on the quiet *cul de sac*, shattering the driver's side window and blowing out the front tire. Jesse screamed in pain and gunned the engine, pressing them into the seats. Craig leaned over Jesse and fired his gun out the broken glass. Two more booming shots answered, and Craig jerked away from Jesse, hitting his head hard on the roof, yelling as if he was on fire. His hand grabbed the wheel. Jesse tried to regain control.

The Denali's headlights and grill were ripped away by a brick mailbox a moment before the entire frontend wrapped around the corner of a house. Fragments of plastic, metal and mortar pelted the door and windows of the home, steam rising from the ruined engine in illuminated wisps that dissipated under the carport.

The impact nearly tore off what was left of her shoulders. The floorboard vibrated from the redlining engine. Craning her neck she could see between the front seats. Craig was hammering his gun down on the airbag ballooned over his lap, shouting for Jesse to get out. He stopped, yanked off his ski mask with a choked gasp, and rivulets of blood streaked across the white canvas airbag.

"Hands! Put your hands on the roof, Craig!"

Chief Perez' command prefaced the entry of a long shotgun barrel into the SUV's interior. Mercie looked up at the gun, realized the window had shattered and covered her with tinted glass.

What is it with me and car wrecks lately?

Chief Petez waited until Craig did as directed. "Now, slowly, drop the gun out on the ground." The shotgun inched in a little more. Craig's growling whine dotted the airbag with more blood. The gun bumped on the ground near the door.

The shotgun disappeared, Chief Perez stepped over to the driver's door and rammed the barrel into the back of Jesse's head. A nasal groan came from deep in the driver's side airbag. Mercie would have grinned if her lips were free.

"Officer MacIntyre," Chief Perez said, breathing hard. "I heard everything. Saw everything. You don't know how close I was to painting Miss Hillbrook's walls with your shit for brains."

Jesse responded with a strangled, pain-filled attempt to suck air into his lungs. Craig turned his face away, looking at the wreckage of the carport.

"Miss Hillbrook? Can you hear me?"

"Mmmngh!"

"Help is coming. I'm calling emergency services

now."

"Ommnkey!"

Now? Now you call for help?

She wanted to yell for Kermit but wasn't sure he was even in the vehicle. Someone scrambled around in the cargo area behind her and she sighed, let her head fall back. Glass crunched into her scalp. She laughed.

Chief Perez' voice took on a calm disgust. "Two of my own. Officers that I personally trained and entrusted the community to." Mercie sensed he was once more considering making paint out of their shit for brains. He continued. "Wait until Judge Stanley sees you in his court, in chains. Shit, and the mayor! You two are about to become serious problems for a bunch of people far above your pay grade." He shifted his grip on the shotgun. Glass crushed under his boots. "What I want to know is, who's pulling your strings? Whose idea was it to murder folks for their assets?"

"Mine."

The Chief shouted and the shotgun barrel hit the roof, going off. The blast inside the SUV was spine jarring. Mercie recovered from the concussion and saw a web of orange embers, the thick roof liner smoldering, smoke choking the men up front.

While Chief Perez was talking Mercie had managed to bend her knees and turn. She pushed off the front seats, rolling her head against the door, slowly working her way onto the seat. A few more kicks and her head cleared the bottom of the window. Glass shards cut deep into her chin. She held in a scream and forced her eyes open. The pain vanished, shock overwhelming her instantly, at the sight of Page MacIntyre plunging a knife into Chief Perez.

The old lawman, stabbed from behind before the

blow to the front, staggered, wrestling the shotgun away from Page. The diminutive woman was a different person than the bank executive Mercie had retaliated against. This version of Page MacIntyre was desperate, viciously berserk, in the way a honey badger will attack a full grown lion - with murderous intent in every swing of her claws.

Mercie jumped as something scorched the numbness of her wrists. She mewled, holding her core firm, easing off the window. Sagging onto the seat she tried to roll. Kermit dropped onto her backside, a weight she welcomed despite bumping her freshly wounded chin.

His butane lighter clicked on, burning her palm.

"Mmmnannagh!" She jerked her hands away. Then realized what he was doing and lay still. "Ommnkay."

"Mnagh!" Kermit said. Arms taped behind him, facing the door, he tried to stop squirming on top of her legs, fingers searching the tape on her wrists. His lighter clicked on again.

This time the mini torch bit deep into the duct tape. It sizzled, tension giving way, popping several layers loose. The strain on her shoulders eased all at once, tape burning through. She yelped, snatched away from the flame. Kermit dropped the lighter and dug into the tape with desperate fingers.

The fight outside rammed into the side of the Denali. Page shouted, "Jesse, wake up! Craig! You useless shit! Help me!" Craig spat a stream of red saliva in answer. He gave up trying to get Jesse to respond to him and went back to fighting the airbag. Arms and legs free, he started to slide out the window, eyes zeroed in on his gun.

Kermit moved faster. Scooted forward onto her lower legs and yanked a big section of tape off.

The fire returned to her shoulders as she eased them forward. Sensation returned in a flood of prickling agony. A glance at Craig and panic fueled her arms to life. She turned over and untaped Kermit. He instantly unraveled the tape binding her boots. Seconds later they faced each other, pulled the tape off their mouths. She grabbed the back of his head, pulled him toward her and kissed his forehead. He stared, taking deep breaths, mouth open.

"Remember what I told you about smoking? About your lighter?" she said.

"Yeah."

"Well, I was wrong. Smoke all you want with that badass lighter. It's the coolest lighter since the Marlboro Man days."

His crooked grinned beamed through the smoke pouring down from the smoldering headliner.

"Let's scram." She followed him out the passenger door. They saw Craig pick up his gun. He looked at them but was on the verge of vomiting, concussed, half his face a giant, swollen bruise that leaked from glass cuts. His ski mask gone, Mercie recognized the man from his newspaper photo. Though, without the uniform for camouflage, she saw his true nature.

Cretin, she thought, grabbing Kermit's shoulders, willing blood back into her feet.

Craig leaned down intending to pick up his gun. Then realized it was already in his hand. Held up the Sig and blinked at it. His strange growl-whine ululated, other hand pressed to his ribs. His murky perception seemed to clear somewhat. Head whipped up, rubbery features contorting with hatred.

"Scram - we gotta scram, bud!" Keeping hold of his shirt she yanked him into her, spun and lunged behind the Denali. Smashed him into the bumper.

"Ow!"

"Sorry", she breathed, thinking the same thing.

Chief Perez was lying beside his shotgun on the grass, chunks of red bricks fanned out around his still form.

"Help, damn you." Page continued shrieking, her head inside the driver's side window. "He's your *partner,* Craig. Help me get him out."

Mercie looked down to whisper to Kermit. He was gone. She turned in a circle, panic hammering. Spotted him sneaking in a wide, quick loop around the yard. He stepped over Chief Perez, grabbed the shotgun, and ran toward the side of the house. He stopped and waved at her.

She focused on not falling on her face and stumbled from behind the SUV. Page's head snapped around. Their eyes locked, and Mercie knew the true depths of this woman's malignant nature. Sweat beaded her entire body in response. Page shouted, flailing at her brother. She pushed away from him, hands gripped in tight fists at her sides.

Mercie recoiled, her failing stamina stealing energy from her legs. She couldn't drag her eyes away from the otherworldly, malevolent glower Page directed at her, blindly running over the grass. Kermit yelled a warning. She looked down, the tip of her boot snagging on a sprinkler head. Her still-tingling arms weren't fast enough to break her fall.

I could've been an acrobat. She spat, pushing wet grass out of her gums. "Brilliant."

"Come on!" Kermit held the shotgun in both hands, stamping his feet in a driveway three houses down. Sticking the gun to his shoulder he brought it up, barrel swaying as he aimed over her.

Teeth bared, eyes still on Mercie, Page leaned over Chief Perez and ripped her knife loose from his chest. She started forward with bad intentions - and was knocked sideways into the Denali by a blast from the shotgun. Metal caved in, dashed with thick scarlet from her head, ear, cheek and half her face missing.

Mercie looked at her friend. Back to the gory mess that slid off the SUV, slumped dead next to a shiny chrome wheel. She made her feet. Wiped hands on her thighs. Shock couldn't prevent her rueful chuckle. *And I was supposed to save him.*

"Still want to be big like me?" She rasped, lurching onto the street next to him. "Few things you should know. That thing you call running?" She slashed a hand across her throat.

Kermit was staring at the gun held horizontal at his waist, bare feet padding below it. "My stomach doesn't hurt anymore."

"You probably left it in the Denali. I need your phone."

They walked faster as they approached the driveway of her house. Kermit pushed open the front door. He laid the shotgun on the beanbag, found his phone and gave it to her. She dialed 911 and told the lady that answered, "Chief Perez was shot..." The phone dropped away from her ear, confused with what to say after all that had happened. She tried again. "People were shot..." She sighed, tossed the phone on the floor.

"Grab some clothes and food. I'll meet you at the Challenger."

He nodded and picked up the Xbox.

"*Clothes* and *food,* dude."

Dropping it, his grumbled reply sounded like retaliation. "They cut the tires on the Challenger. It's sitting on the ground."

"What? No way." Confusion sank in full force

then. All she could think of was getting them in the car and burning rubber. "*Swell,*" she cursed.

Kermit grabbed some jeans out of a Kohl's box, lay them over a shoulder. He picked up the shotgun and lay it on his other shoulder, little chest pushed out. "Don't worry." He grinned. "We'll take my car."

"You have a car?"

***

"You have a car." Mercie walked into the garage and stopped, blinking at the humongous blue Cadillac filling the space her parents' car normally occupied. *Well, okay, then...* She dumped an armful of clothes in the back and walked around the front.

"I'm driving. It's my car." Offended eyes looked up at her. "You ride shotgun," he said handing her one.

She snatched it from him. "*Ugh.* Drive. Let's just get out of here." Her legs had regained function. Relief a car was in the garage and they could leave, trimmed away the fear. The fresh memory of Page yanking a knife out of Chief Perez - seconds before her head spatter painted the SUV - kept any kind of sigh or smile from forming, however.

Rusted door hinges creaked open, clunked shut. The interior smelled of mold but gave her an immediate feeling of safety. She watched him dig out a long screwdriver and pair of pliers from under the seat. She smirked briefly in response to his nervous glance.

"I thought this was your car."

"It is." Head under the big steering wheel, he flashed a scowl in her direction, grim expression settling into one of determination as he scraped the tools on the side of the steering column. The starter whined, massive engine shifting side to side. A popping roar as it started made her yelp. Exhaust fumes thick with raw fuel filled the car.

Mercie coughed and pulled her shirt over her nose. "Where in the world did you find this thing?"

"Craigslist."

"Of course."

Pulling himself up by the steering wheel, his butt hovered off the seat. Half his body vanished as he stomped down on the brake and shifted, arm jerking as 'reverse' thunked into gear. The big Sedan revved a warbling roar, Kermit piloting it out into the street with the skill of a boat captain fighting a current in a tricky harbor. Tongue poking from the side of his mouth, blue tinted smoke squinting his eyes.

Mercie wanted to look behind them but couldn't. She stared at Kermit and wondered what other impossibilities she would witness before the night was over.

The Caddy's drive train popped and clattered from seemingly everywhere at once. The feeling of safety vanquished with a rumbling belch of flame shooting out of the mufflers. She grabbed the seatbelt. "You know a good place to go?"

He didn't answer. Eyes narrowed, he stabbed a toe at the pedals, dipping under the dashboard and pulling the shifter down with him. The brake went all the way to the floor with a hiss that preceded a grinding halt, pitching her forward. He swept the steering wheel in the other direction, braced with a tight grip and pulled himself back to his hover position. Glanced at her, brows furrowed, and chuffed around his tongue. The old luxury sedan squatted, squealed up and down on thirty year old suspension. Something banged like an alarm bell and she pulled her feet onto the seat.

The car sat there, unmoving, making more racket than a war movie marathon.

She looked through the exhaust haze past Kermit as a shadow moved on the street. She turned and saw it lengthen, pointing right at them. A new spike of terror struck her.

"Kermit..."

He growled, an annoyed exertion one uses on a stubborn dog that refuses to be led by a leash. Yanked on the shifter, arms pulling, legs pressing. The shifter handle resisted, a bow drawn with every muscle. It released, linkage rods firing the transmission into gear with a bang that sent a shiver from bumper to bumper. He revved it before it could stall. They rolled forward.

Mercie started to cheer. A lungful of smoke cut it short.

Kermit growled again, this one accompanied by a mean grin. "She's angry when she's cold," he said with pride, leg easing under the wheel.

She stared at him. Fascinated and suffocated she fanned smoke from her eyes and played with loose, chipped window switches that did absolutely nothing. "She?" Shirt over her nose again, she let her eyes tear and laughed at the crazy frown he turned on her.

"It's a *Cadillac*. It can't be a boy." His serious expression darkened as they passed under a streetlight, quick eyes roving over cars parked by the gutter. The engine revved and sputtered, gears slipping. Mercie almost missed his sulking, "Her name is Miss Piggy."

A small dip on a curve jounced them sharply on the seat. The front end swayed toward a Neighborhood Watch sign. He corrected the slack in the steering, narrowly avoided the burglar warning, and coaxed the big V8 to a thundering shimmy that powered them out of the subdivision at a ferocious 40 mph.

"Sorry we couldn't let you warm up first, Miss Piggy," Mercie said patting the dash. Dry-rotted paint and foam crumbled, stuck to her palm. She turned to Kermit. "She does sound angry." She stroked the dashboard to wipe her hand. "And very tired."

He peered around the interior that was more than twice his age. "I'm gonna fix her up." Miss Piggy faltered, backfired, and then caught power again.

Kermit's eyes widened. He looked at Mercie and they burst out laughing.

"Bud, I admire a man that's loyal to his girl."

"Huh?"

"You'll get it one day. You'll be broke, but Miss Piggy will be nice looking."

"Huh?"

They laughed again.

Miss Piggy's anger and their shock-laced humor masked the approach of the car barreling over a hill at suicidal speed. The Saab's tires chirped through two intersections, the whine of the engine revving higher. Mercie's heightened sense of danger jerked her face to the window.

Light traced over Page's Saab in reflective strobes, blinking on the face of the driver, the gun held on the steering wheel.

"Kermit! *Go!*"

Panic dragged on the terrible pace of the moment. Kermit's leg jabbed down. Before Miss Piggy could respond, Craig's blood matted features and bared teeth registered in Mercie's new dose of shock.

The Saab rammed into the Cadillac. The impact smashed Kermit into Mercie, and her into the door pillar. The concussion deafened them, fragments of safety glass spraying soundless in the same forced direction, covering their contorted forms. The cars whirled in a deadly tango, g-forces gripping, pinning bodies and stealing conscious thought.

The Cadillac's tonnage, Saab attached to its side, crushed a concrete curb, shrieking tires exploding with shards of cement. Bare wheels plowed deep furrows into a slope, city planted sod shooting up in waves that rained down in clumps.

The ground quaked under them. Kermit screamed against Mercie's neck as the slide continued. The soft earth hardly slowed the wreck. The angle of the bank steepened, then fell away into a gully.

The force of the spinning slide lessened, Kermit fell away, then smacked hard into the roof, head then legs. Anti-freeze steamed onto her weightless limbs, gushed over her shoulders, hair, cars rolling, bouncing off the bank. Her arms whipped into the roof, seat, and dashboard, into her face... a second of zero gravity... then her breath and vision were crushed into oblivion.

The wreck landed on a man-made cliff, on a central drain. The pipe underneath resounded with a thunderous punch that shook the road above. Spots of plasma glowed briefly on the steel grating that took the weight, Cadillac welding to it. Mercie sucked in a breath and heard a masculine yell sail overhead. She pictured Tarzan with tiger jaws buried in his spine and flinched as it ended with a burst of glass. The Saab pole-vaulted over the drain, tore loose from the Cadillac. Flipped end over end down the gradient.

Craig's psychotic, scarlet face was imprinted on Mercie's closed eyes. Wrinkles in her forehead deepened with the booming metallic rattle of the Saab flipping down the hill.

A burning bloomed all over her, torturing away the dizziness. *Get out you moron! The car's on fire!* Reality clarified with the pain of scalded skin, the smell of anti-freeze, and she remembered to breathe. *The car isn't burning. I am... Where's Kermit?*

"Mercie? Mercie!"

His voice, the relief from hearing it, chased away the dregs of unconsciousness. Unclenching her eyes, she nearly screamed. Her scorched eyelids signaled a wave of hurt, nerves reporting horrific injury across her scalp, neck, down the center of her back.

"*Mercie...*"

"What?"

"Get off of me."

Jaw clenched, she twisted her arm, pulled it from in front of her face, eyes crossing as she saw Kermit balled up, smashed under the steering wheel. "Oh. You okay?"

"No. Miss Piggy will need a lot more fixing up now."

"Sorry, bud. I think you should consider that love affair over with." Tears welled in his eyes. She flapped a hand. "Don't worry! There are plenty more where she came from."

Gently shutting her eyes, she pawed the door, the floorboard, pushed up. "That *shit weasel.*"

"Who?" He slivered almost boneless around her, grabbed a hole in the dashboard that once held an A/C control panel. Maneuvered over into the backseat.

"Craig. The ass-hat that hit us."

"Wasn't that the bank lady's car?"

"Yeah. How did you know?"

"I stole her stereo before you caught me stealing yours."

"Ow. Ow. Stop." She stuck a palm up. "Don't

torture me with that awesome story yet. Let me get some ice first."

"Craig."

"Yeah. He was one of the cops that killed my parents." Groaning, she held her core firm, drew up her knees. Gripped the wheel and planted her feet down where her head had been. Straightening her back wasn't happening. Tender skin rebelled, forced a crouch that made breathing a life or death task. She gave herself a mental pat on the back for not vomiting and passing out. Then whispered, "His partner was the bank lady's brother. The shit weasel that stuffed us in the Denali." He didn't reply or move. She began laboring herself in a careful turn. "Neither of them are a danger anymore, though, alright? Jesse looked dead in the Denali, and Craig just went flipping down that hill. No way he's getting up from that."

"No… *Craig.*"

"Yeah. *Craig.* The douche canoe that just went *cirque de sole* in Page's fancy bank salary car." Arm over the seatback, she froze and rode the burn. Focused on him and said through clenched teeth, "What's wrong? Are you hurt?"

He stared straight up, mouth slack. He muttered, "The douche canoe didn't go suck dude so lay in Page's car."

Her neck shrank into her shoulders as fine scorched fuzz on the back of it jumped up, chill racing over. She realized what was wrong a heartbeat before she felt his eyes.

"Hey Misty," Craig said, looking down on them from atop the passenger door. He shifted into shadow. An eerie glow outlined him from the lights lining the main road. His knees caved in the side of the door, and engine oil, warm and thick, streamed down on their upturned faces.

Ducking, Mercie wiped her eyes then looked over at Kermit. His face was painted red.

"You want some more of that?" Craig stood, held his leg over the hole in the busted window and shook it. Blood ran off his boot and pants, showered into the car. The whites of his eyes, alight with that eerie luminescence, rolled to her. "I'll mix yours with it in a second." His gun came into view, pointing at Kermit. "Then I'll use it as lube on the boy."

She didn't duck as more blood dripped down, paralyzed by the gun directed at her head. Craig waivered on the unsteady door but his gun arm didn't. Ugly hatred tore at his features, lips disappearing from around gritted teeth. His hand jabbed down as his finger tightened on the trigger.

A tongue of flame exploded up from the backseat, volcanic in the confines of the interior. It punched large holes in the door under Craig, smoke boiling out around him.

A ringing pressure hummed in Mercie's temples, fingers pressed deep into the seat cushion. A sob bubbled on her lips. She screamed, "Kermit!" and vomited, ringing pressure overwhelming her senses. Struggling, desperate eyes searched the door above, jerking to the backseat. The barrel of the shotgun rose to aim at the door, and she followed it down to see her friend standing where the backseat should have been, butt of the gun braced against the vertical floorboard. He looked at her and said something impossible to hear but was felt with all of her heart.

Her body was trying to shut down. Straightening made acidic bile rise in her throat. It spilled from the corners of her mouth, legs pushing her over the seat.

Kermit's tiny arms shook with the weight of the weapon. His eyes flickered to her, back to the door where Craig had disappeared from in a magician-like poof of smoke. A gush of wind cleared the window and holes, starless sky above black with the promise of more lethal surprises.

Mercie touched Kermit's leg. He looked and nodded at her gesture to climb out. The back door was completely unrecognizable, wrapped around the rear wheel. The central pillar and part of the roof had torn away. Kermit handed her the gun and climbed through the jagged slot, climbed on top of the shotgun blasted door and hurried to take the weapon back from her.

The ringing lessened. The Cadillac squeaked and groaned into a precarious lean with their weight on its side. Mercie chose not to climb on top, negotiating over the jagged metal with shaking hands, pulse beating hard at her neck.

"I don't see him," Kermit shouted.

The car rocked away from her as she jumped down. The grating under her boots moved up and down, a wave of tense steel. Balancing with hands running along the roof made moving to the front of the Cadillac possible. She looked up at Kermit. He turned with the gun pointed at the ground on the other side. Spun his head around to tell her, "He's dead. He's gotta be, right?"

The pistol sounded like a firecracker popping after the deafening shotgun blast. Kermit jerked and backpedaled, dropped the shotgun and fell off the front of the car.

Mercie heard his grunt, hitting the grate hard, and made herself move, rounding the car. She found Kermit, his legs sticking out in front of the sod covered bumper, the rest of him off the side of the drain, in the dark grass. Lurching away from the wreck she fell down trying to pick up the shotgun. A sob burst out and choked her.

"There you are. Hey boy. Get up. It's no fun if you don't fight back."

Craig's sick words floated up from the slope. Mercie's entire body shook. Terror became rage, weak limbs digging for new strength. Using the gun as a cane, she staggered up, lifted the barrel and marched toward Craig's wheeze determined to protect her friend with no thought of the risk.

"Where's Misty? Huh, boy? Where is that stupid fat bitch?" Craig crawled through the grass on his elbows, clothes soaked with muddy blood, face smeared with it. He climbed up the underside of the Cadillac, peering around the hoodless engine. He brought his weapon up by his chin and stepped over Kermit's feet to point and shoot.

Mercie shouted, the shotgun barrel stabbing Craig in the face. She forgot to pull the trigger, falling into him. Craig dropped his gun and grabbed a piece of tire still on the front wheel. They pitched over.

The Cadillac went with them.

Mercie continued shouting as darkness descended, car crashing down on them. The crunch went silent and she found herself facedown in thick grass still shouting. Something twisted her head around, pain flaring from her scalp.

"Got you." Craig spat, started coughing.

Mercie tried to pull away, but his grip on her hair was too strong. She dug nails into his hands with everything she had.

He burped a laugh. "Yes! That's how I like it."

Her eyes darted to the sides. Back to him. A pink froth bubbled from his mouth, manic eyes boring into her. She looked behind him and couldn't see anything, realizing the blackness was the car on top of him.

Is it on me, too?

Her mind raced, finding no answers. She could move her legs and arms, but couldn't pry free. The car shifted above her, panic stealing her air, and she knew it would crush them both any second.

She thrashed and yanked her head in every direction.

"Oh, no you don't." The lock of hair slipped in his grasp then held firm. "Not happening, Misty," he croaked.

Kermit yelled a warning, swinging down from the bumper. His heel struck Craig in the eye, a solid, fleshy thud. All of them cried out at once. Mercie and Kermit scrambled away and collapsed on their stomachs, gasping.

The car shifted then stopped, rocking in place.

Kermit helped her up. They approached and looked under what was left of Miss Piggy. Craig's wheezing had become uncontrollable coughing. He glanced at them, his attention focused on the object that was keeping the engine and transmission from making pulp out of his head.

The shotgun.

Mercie tilted her head, studying the pitiful creature that had been a murderous animal moments ago. She leaned down, grabbed the top of the shotgun barrel, and studied the bumper sitting on it.

"I was the one that shot your mother." Craig's head snapped side to side with a disturbing cackle. He spat and grabbed at the butt of the gun just out of reach. "I saw her head pop like a shook up Budweiser."

She pulled on the barrel, then paused.

"You don't have the spine for it, you sow. You won't kill me." He looked to the side, listening to a train of sirens coming their way. "I'll live. And then you won't." He spat blood at them. "Fuck you, boy. Fuck *you,* Misty."

"Her name is Mercie!" Kermit said.

"And I have none for you."
She snatched the barrel free.

***

The blinding flashes and deafening sirens weren't the problem. She could ignore the burn deep in her shoulders, turning numb from her hands once more bound behind her. It was her eyes and nose - they itched like mad. Fear of re-opening the gash on her chin kept her stock-still in the backseat of the police cruiser.

Her pulse had slowed enough for exhaustion to take her. Beginning to nod, she heard a familiar, impossible voice, and forced her eyes to stay open.

His ghost, too? Ugh. First Mom, now this guy…

"She should be in a fucking ambulance," said the ghost on a police radio. "The boy, too!"

"Sir, she's out on bail for bank robbery." The tall black police officer standing next to her locked door held a radio to his lips, rubbing the back of his neck. "There will be more charges. Maybe capital murder. And likely no bail."

"We don't have time for this bullshit. You take that lady to the hospital, now. In a fucking ambulance."

Before her eyelids betrayed her, she saw the officer glance around and hit the radio on his leg. He left it at his side and said, "Ten-four."

The seat creaked as she leaned back on the door. Eyes rolled back, mouth slack, she jerked upright and shouted. The center of her chest burned as she saw the knife tore loose from Chief Perez' chest.

***

"Wake the hell up, lady."

"Hey man! Be nicer. She's hurt really damn bad, you know."

"I want to go back to my room really damn bad. You know." Something squeaked on the floor. "How the hell are you even standing?"

"Standing? Man, I could run! I mean... Not *from* you. But that I could if I wanted..."

Police Chief Perez coughed a chuckle. Groaning he said, "I know what you mean, boy."

"Kermit."

The squeak again. "Uh-huh. Kermit, you say? It's the drugs, Kermit. In reality, you are nearly dead. Me, well, I should *be* dead. Drugs, boy, have separated us from the reality of painful handicaps. You can't run. The drugs just make you feel like you can."

"Oh. Then I like drugs. I like feeling like I can run."

"Perez. When you retire, stay away from substance abuse groups. With kids, just keep it simple. Try the 'Just Say No' slogan. God you suck."

"That's *Chief* Perez." He grinned up from his wheelchair. "How you feeling?"

Mercie had to turn her head to see the room; moving her eyes hurt too bad. Perez sat a few feet from her bed, a massive bandage wrapped around his upper body. His face was stern as usual, though his glasses shined with bright twinkling eyes behind the shaded lens.

She stuck a hand out to ward off Kermit's hug. "Squeeze me and it won't be pretty."

"Ha ha. Want me to get us some tacos?" He sat at the foot of the bed. His blue gown glowed against the new white sheet covering her feet.

"Shit no. *Barf.* Shut up dude. No taco talk for a week at least." Her head shifted to look at him. "You can hug me then. After we talk about drugs."

He nodded. "I like drugs."

"No. You don't."

The corner of her mouth felt torn. She dabbed her tongue at it, tasted blood. Put a finger to her stiff cheek and discovered scabbed lacerations all over. She grimaced and spoke carefully. "I saw you Perez. You were…"

"Taken out by a Chihuahua in a skirt? Yeah, I know it was bad. The boys will crucify me when I get back to the station." He wheezed, leaned over. "The girls, too. Shit."

"When I re-tell it I'll beef her up. Make her a rabid gym freak."

"Will you? I'd appreciate that."

Their laughs wheezed into groans and gasps. Perez tapped the bandage encasing his chest. "Pacemaker. Deflected the blade. I used to hate the damn thing. Every day it reminded me of my impending death. Now I'm thinking I'm fucking immortal. Might quit the desk job and hit the field again."

"Really? Like chase bad guys?" Kermit stared in disbelief. "Your hair is white. And you're all wrinkled."

"So was Dirty Harry." He looked at Mercie. "What's wrong with him?"

"You're white, he's Vietnamese. Sarcasm language barrier. Plus, you're all wrinkled and he can run on drugs."

Kermit looked from Mercie to Chief Perez and nodded. "I could run if I had to."

"Let's hope you don't have to." Chief Perez wheeled his chair around to look at the door. "Kermit, will you close that please? If I roll over there I might run out of gas. We need to discuss a few things while I'm able."

"Take more drugs," Kermit advised, walking past to shut the door. Returned to his seat.

"Ha. I just might."

"What is there to discuss? I'm going to prison. You'll get an award. Key to the city, maybe. Something special to hang on your wall." Her tongue poked at the scab covering her upper lip, eyes downcast.

"What? She's going to prison?" Kermit leapt to his feet, loose paper gown puffing out from his skinny legs. "You can do something, right? She won't have to go, right?"

"Bud, this isn't like the movies. He can't change the law. He has to enforce it. That's his job. He can't do anything for me."

"Yes. I can."

They looked at him. Mercie said, "Can what? Yes what?"

"Told you! I knew he could." Kermit grinned at her.

"Can and will." He sighed through his nose, adjusted his glasses. "This stays between us three. Got that?" He stared at them in turn. They nodded, silent. "The DA owes me one. He was hot shit in Jackson. Took a job here I helped him get. He's also my nephew. What that means is – "

"I know what it means." Mercie wiped the corners of her eyes. Whispered, "Thank you."

Perez leaned toward her. "I can get the armed robbery reduced. You'll be on probation for a few years. After the investigation you'll get the house back. Your folks' belongings, well, I doubt you'll ever see that again. You could sue…"

"But then you couldn't help me. I'll go to prison."

He nodded. "Five years, minimum."

"Don't sue, Mercie. We can buy new belongings, just like your parents had in the house. I don't want you to go to prison." Kermit looked at his friend, terrified by the thought.

She nodded and patted Kermit's hand. "We got justice for my mom and dad. I'm not suing the city."

"Damn right you got justice. And you have the money to furnish the house." He took off his glasses, rubbed them clean on his gown. "I'm going to be an asshole and say it's not compensation for the loss of your folks. But it's all the compensation you're going to get."

"What money?" Mercie's head lifted, turned to him. "Kermit, wheel him back to his room. His hair is too white, he's got too many wrinkles. Old and senile."

Kermit stepped around the wheelchair, gripped the handles. Perez never broke eye contact with Mercie. He set the brakes on the wheels and said, "The *bank money*, lady."

She fumbled with the nurse call button. "Oh, wow. The *pain*. I have to rest…"

"Oh. Haha." Kermit looked at her, smiling.

Chief Perez turned red trying not to laugh. Taking a deep breath he rubbed his chest. "We have a deal? Probation. Don't sue… and keep the cash. I need you both to say yes then never say anything about it ever again."

"Yes."

"Yes."

"Good. Grand. Now, boy, wheel my old ass back to my room. You're going to help me take a crap then tell the nurse I need more drugs."

"Huh?" Kermit looked at Mercie, wide eyed. She shrugged.

"Oh. Wait. One more thing." Chief Perez put his glasses on and squinted up at Mercie. "Who's Challenger was that in your driveway? You owe my wife a damn car."

Re-Pete

One eye was stuck wide open. Dry, angry red veins, thick behind the eyelids, branched out to thin tendrils that appeared to tease a scarred iris.

Above the eye, the paralysis had seized the brow into a thick black arch that sloped all the way across a face that rarely saw sunlight.

The other eye was functional. It was stuck half-closed, watered incessantly, and was sort of... *bent.* But he could see out of it most of the time.

Pete ran a finger under his eye, swiped it on his shirt. His face unblurred in the mirror. He continued brushing his teeth. As Aqua fresh spittle accumulated on his reflection he stared at his scarred iris, unable to look away. His heart beat faster. His throat tightened. Breaths coming in short gasps through his nose, toothbrush tearing hard and fast on his teeth, Pete leaned forward and pressed his forehead to the bottom of the mirror until he couldn't see himself any longer. Short gasp as the toothbrush popped out, a huge sharp breath. He spat into the sink with a shout. The toothbrush clattered in the sink basin.

Pete lost his balance and fell to the floor.

A shadow fell across him. "Pete?"

"I'm okay, Mother."

"Sure, Pete. Sure. You look okay."

Pete wiped sweat from his forehead and sat up. He jumped as the toilet flushed behind him. Looked up and relaxed at the sight of his mother's smile.

In a soft, quiet voice she said, "You didn't flush or put the seat down." The toilet seat and lid slammed hard in the small, tiled room. "Wipe the mirror."

"Yes, Mother. I was going to flush the toilet."

"Sure, Pete. I know you were."

In the hallway a bedroom door opened, booted

steps approached on the linoleum. "Hey Bev. That fucking idiot do it again?" A man filled the bathroom doorway, head and shoulders brushing the frame. His old cowboy boots thumped to a widespread stop. He displayed large teeth, looked down at Pete. "You little pussy. You're scared of your own reflection. *Every fucking day.*"

"Eagle!" Bev moved to stand in front of the man. "That's not helping. That's not how it works. He has severe obsessive compulsive disorder. He's been diagnosed."

"Yeah, he's made it clear he's severely disordered. But you're the one obsessed with it."

Pete wrapped his arms around his legs. Buried his face between his knees.

Bev clucked her tongue, glanced at her son. "Talking to him like that only makes it worse."

Eagle ran a hand over his facial stub, glaring at the two. He raised his voice. "No, talking to him like that will toughen up his little ass." He narrowed his dark eyes. "And talking to *me* like that will get *your* ass toughened up. Go make me some coffee, Bev, before I make you scared of your own reflection."

Bev closed her mouth and dropped her eyes. She pressed her lips together and shuffled past Eagle into the hallway.

Eagle smiled after her. Turned to Pete. "Your daddy ain't around here to coddle you and your mother anymore, boy. And I ain't gonna be the man of a weak family. You hear me?" He leaned down and gripped Pete's shoulder hard. Shook him. "You better toughen up if you know what's best for you…" He jerked his head toward the hallway. "And your mom."

Pete fell over when the big man let go and left the bathroom. He wiped his eye and stood. Peered through the doorway, holding his breath. A drop of water splat in the sink and he gasped, looked around wildly. Looked at the mirror and the Aqua fresh spittle.

Grabbing a roll of paper towels from under the sink, he tore off a couple and started to wipe the mirror. One quick swipe and his reflection smeared. He let out a breath. He repositioned the paper towel and tried to keep breathing as he leaned over the sink to wipe again.

As his hand inched closer he tried to keep focused on the smeared spittle and ignore his paralyzed eye growing larger in front of him. Sweat trickled down his sides from his armpits. His fingers pressed the paper towel to the mirror but his hand wouldn't make the wiping motion; it only trembled.

Eagle cursed Bev in the front room - he scalded his lips with 'her' coffee - and Pete squeaked in pain as his elbow hit the sink. He held his breath and ran from the bathroom.

***

"He's a 'repeater'. So recurring obsessions are not abnormal." The doctor turned off his optic scope and focused on holding a neutral expression. He glanced at Pete, knowing the kid sensed his disgust, gave a small smile, and then turned to the mother. "The experience that caused the disorder, and consequently the paralysis, was extremely traumatic. And relatively recent."

Bev fiddled with her purse strap. She hated examination rooms. Hated *hospitals*. She uncrossed her legs, stood and smoothed the back of her shirt over her shorts. Shouldered her purse. "I don't know why I even bring him here. It seems like I've spent my entire life in this place. Certainly spent my life *savings*… I give up."

The doctor frowned, adjusted his glasses. "Your

son's diagnosis is not one that can be healed with a prescription or home remedy. I've personally never administered to a patient with such severe OCD. For mild OCD, *Prozac* or *Wellbutrin* works fine to inhibit compulsions and repetitive behavior. Time and understanding - *patience* - is what Pete needs. And you are giving that to him."

"I got it." Bev motioned for Pete to get off the table. He slid down, turned and grabbed his shirt. Pulled it over his head, watching his mom. She folded her arms and sighed. "Except for the patience part. My patience these days is *shit.*"

"Well Ms…" He held up a clipboard.

"Bev. Just Bev. Hello? I'm here three times a month and you still don't know my name?"

"Well Bev." He cleared his throat. "The brain is a wondrous organ. The plasticity allows damaged neural pathways to find new paths. Keep doing the eye exercises, and one day the eye may regain some functionality. The discipline of the physical exercises may help alleviate the OCD. It's a long-term solution, but it's the only solution in today's medicine."

"That's your opinion," Bev muttered.

"Excuse me?"

"Thanks for your opinion."

He frowned. "Ah, also, as to the, ah," he glanced at Pete, "inconvenience of his recurring obsession, that also may change with time. That particular behavior may cease altogether. But most likely it will be replaced with another, sometimes similar, act."

"Another? Are you fuc - " Bev looked at her son, who continued to stare at her. She put a stick of gum in her mouth, stuck the pack back in her purse. Tried not to glare at the doctor and chewed while talking. "Are you seriously telling me this right now? *Another* obsession? How? What can I expect?"

A group of nurses walked quickly past the exam room. One turned back and knocked before opening the door. "Doctor," she said with quiet urgency.

"Sure." He looked at Bev and Pete as he backed out of the room. "Expect? Hell if I know." He chuckled. "That's part of the fun." With a big grin he was gone.

What a fucking asshole. Bev scowled, stroking Pete's hair. *I swear, I should go slash his tires…*

Pete swiped his eye and kept watching his mother's face.

***

Pete didn't like sleeping with the lights off. He didn't like the *quiet* of dark. And didn't understand why his parents always made a fuss about making the whole house dark and quiet before bed. It made him scared, not sleepy. And it made his parents mad at him because he talked or got out of bed to play with his toys by the light coming through the window.

They got *really* mad when they had to keep getting out of bed to come into his room to shush him or yell at him for playing when he should be sleeping. So they made him sleep with them most nights. But he didn't really sleep.

How could he sleep when it was so quiet and dark?

Since Daddy had gone to Heaven and the big man became his new daddy he didn't sleep in his parents' room anymore. So he slept in his own bed, and Mother didn't check to see if he was playing by the window. And whenever he got scared and talked about things the big man just yelled instead of coming to his room like Daddy used to.

Pete didn't like the yelling. But he was glad he didn't have to sleep with Mother and the big man.

He went to his room. He was very tired after the doctor visit. The hospital was a scary place. Every time Mother drove them to see the doctor Pete saw people that were hurt. Most of them were hurt so bad they were in beds - and those same people would be in the same beds the next time Mother drove them to see the doctor! *That* scared Pete, too.

The only thing Pete liked about visiting the doctor was the nice ladies in pyjamas. They were very nice because they didn't make fun of his face. And they had some *really cool* pyjamas!

Pete climbed onto his bed and pulled a race car from under his pillow. He rolled it back and forth over his stomach, wishing he had pyjamas like they did…

The nice ladies told him how handsome he looked in his new Scooby Doo pyjamas. He smiled at the cartoon dog that was all over his arms, his stomach and legs. He laughed with the nice ladies.

One of the nice ladies stepped in front of the others. She became so big the other nice ladies disappeared. Her laugh hurt his ears. He cupped his hands over his ears and pushed the sound away. He closed his eyes.

In the darkness the nice lady stopped laughing. Pete couldn't see her but knew she was gone… And he wasn't at the doctor visit anymore. He was at home. In his parent's room. Daddy was sleeping next to him; Pete always knew when Daddy was sleeping because he made funny noises with his nose. He liked how Daddy always smelled like his truck. Mother wasn't in bed. He knew when she was gone because he got cold and had to get all the way under the sheet. Sometimes she left after Daddy started making funny noises. Pete didn't understand why she left. He liked the funny noises. Hearing them made him sleepy and made the scary quiet go away.

Pete tried to move closer to Daddy but couldn't find him. The whole bed was cold. And the scary quiet came back. Pete sat up when the hallway light came on. It was bright under the bedroom door and hurt his eyes. Two shadows appeared in the middle of the light like missing front teeth. The shadows moved wide right before the door crashed open. A huge black bear stomped into the room holding his paws out to his sides. The bear growled and turned its head. Pete saw it was a very big man, and he was very mad.

Daddy was making funny noises again. Pete sighed as the scary quiet left and looked at the bedroom door. It was closed. The bear hadn't broken it down. Pete scooted over to curl up behind Daddy and the door crashed open.

Daddy shouted, "Who is that? Who are you?" and leapt from the bed. "Where's Bev? BEV!"

Daddy grabbed for his pants off the dresser. The big man stepped in and hit Daddy really hard in the face. He fell onto the table next to the bed, crushing a lamp.

Pete pulled the covers over his head. He couldn't breathe. The men fought on the floor, upending the chair and table, shoving the dresser into the door. Makeup, coins scattered, and old magazines were shredded under their legs.

Pete shouted, "Mother!" and scrambled off the bed away from the scary fight. He got under the bed, pulling the sheets with him.

"Fucking my girl!" the big man thundered, punching Daddy.

Daddy growled in pain and turned the big man over on top of the bed. Something cracked and the bed suddenly smashed down on Pete. He shouted for Mother then couldn't breathe. He shut his eyes tight. Above him legs kicked the walls then he could breath as the men thumped over on the floor. He opened his eyes. Right in front of his face Daddy lay with the big man on top of him. Daddy was shaking bad, spitting huge breaths, but couldn't push the big man off.

The big man roared and Pete saw the huge bear lean over Daddy. Light coming through the busted door made the long blade gripped in the bear's paws shine. It quivered and the paws became hands pushing down. Daddy yelped like a puppy that had been stepped on, then yelled loud as the big knife pressed into his chest.

The big man's eyes were wide and shaking. His lips, wet and open, showed large white teeth. "Fucking my girl? Huh? DID YOU FUCK MY GIRL?"

"No!" Daddy yelped.

"No? That's what she said. At first." The big man sat up. He slowly pulled the knife out of Daddy.

Pete, unable to close his eyes, heard a sound like his foot being pulled out of thick mud. The mud turned as red as Daddy's blood on the knife.

"Tell me how you did my girl." The big man pushed down again. Daddy screamed a sound that made Pete start panting. Pete saw the blade slowly bite into Daddy's chest again. Daddy's arms poured sweat, feebly pushing at the big man's hands.

"It wasn't me... wasn't me!" Daddy said. "I - " He gasped as the blade twisted. His legs, under the big man, kicked and slammed his heels hard on the floor.

"You fucked her! You fucked her!" The big man's spit sprayed all over Daddy's face. "You did! She told me you did!"

The red mud appeared, Pete's foot dragging clear...

The point of the knife disappeared into Daddy's side. Pete was becoming dizzy. His throat pulsed, sucking in small wheezes of air. He watched Daddy scoot around, squealing. Daddy's hand fumbled over Pete's face and squeezed it. Pete wheezed louder, eyes staring through Daddy's fingers. The hand let go, pushing at the bed.

The big man put a hand over Daddy's mouth. The squealing stopped. Their noses almost touched. The big man shouted, "Tell me how you did it! Tell me!" He twisted the knife.

Daddy made a sound like a big frog, then he hummed against the big man's hand. The light coming into the room made the tears in Daddy's eyes turn yellow. The bear paw moved off his mouth. "I'm sorry!" Daddy said.

"Sorry? That's the same fucking thing she said. Sorry. You two were made for each other. Two sorry motherfuckers!"

"I am. I'm really sorry." Just like Pete, Daddy couldn't breathe right. "It just… happened."

The bear sat up and roared. Then he slammed the knife into Daddy's head. It sounded like a big watermelon when Mother stuck her "good" knife in it. Pete liked watermelon.

Pete's panting slowed. His eyebrows felt funny. And one eye hurt really bad because it wouldn't close. He saw Daddy's stomach stop moving. Then his mouth stopped moving…

Pete saw himself as he did every morning in the bathroom and started panting fast again.

***

Pete walked out of his bedroom holding his favorite toy: a big fire truck, the kind with real lights and a siren that works and a ladder that moves up and down like a real ladder. He didn't play with it last night by the window. But he wanted to.

The fire truck was longer than his arm. He carried it with both hands, keeping an eye on the ladder. Sometimes it shot out and scraped the wall. Mother got angry when his toys scraped the walls. Pete knew it was because the big man gets really mad at her whenever Pete makes a mess or breaks something.

He held the fire truck in front of him whenever there were no lights on in the hallway. Pete could just use the lights on the fire truck. He saw the bathroom light was already on and turned to carefully place his favoritest toy back in his room.

As he walked into the bathroom he noticed his hand didn't shake when he pushed the door. He stared at the doorknob, knowing it would make his hand shake. But it didn't. He wiggled his fingers and frowned. He wanted to keep watching the doorknob but he had to pee *really* bad!

He finished and flushed the toilet, put the seat down. Turning to the sink he looked up at his reflection: big ears sticking out of long dark hair that covered his funny eyebrows and the eye that wouldn't close. He didn't like his hair long, in his face. Mother wanted it like that. She said he embarrassed her.

The sink had tiny hairs all over it from the big man's beard. Pete wrinkled his nose, grabbed some paper towels and wiped it clean. Then he brushed his teeth. Leaning forward, he watched his teeth and gums closely to make sure the toothbrush moved the way Daddy showed him.

Rinsed his mouth, cleaned his Scooby Doo toothbrush, and looked at the mirror. He was surprised he didn't have to wipe it clean. He shrugged and went back to his room to play with the fire truck.

***

Bev heard her son in the bathroom and sighed. Blew out a breath and grabbed Eagle's coffee mug off the TV - *the TV!* - and walked into the kitchen. Stopped at the sink. Bracelets jingled as she swept her long dark hair back into a ponytail. She grabbed the sink sprayer and began washing the mug. Her cheekbones poked out, lips pursed. Tiny wrinkles sprang from narrowed eyes. *On top of the fucking TV... Eagle is such a dick.* She shook her head. *It's a nice dick, but that's all the fuckhead is good for.*

Wiping down the counter she heard Pete's fire truck siren blaring. She stopped, frowning. Then went to the laundry room to trade out towels on the way to check on Pete's daily bathroom crap.

"Huh. Son of a bitch." Bev stood in the bathroom doorway looking around with her mouth open. The toilet seat was down. The mirror was clean. And he had even cleaned Eagle's bullshit out of the sink. "I'll be damned."

As Bev walked over to Pete's room she remembered what the doctor had said. She hoped whatever new crap he started was better than the old crap. Easier to clean up.

And she hoped whatever new crap he started wouldn't piss off Eagle… or give him a new reason to hurt her.

***

"Just watch him. I'll be back in a few hours."

"Watch him do what?"

"You know what I mean. He's sleeping. You don't have to actually watch him. Just be here in case something happens."

"Oh, yeah, because this is the place where things happen. What could possibly happen in this little Disney dump?"

"Just stay, Eagle. Damn. It's my uncle's funeral. He was a good man and I'm going to see his family. And there's no way in hell I'm bringing you or Pete. I'll be embarrassed enough on my own."

"I don't want to stay. The boys are still at the bar. It's two-for-one night, and I just got that new cue…"

"Let go. Stop, Eagle!"

"Well, if I can't have beer and play pool I wanna play with you."

"*No.* I have to go. We can do that in the morning when Pete has his bath."

"Ah shit, Bev. That's the only thing worth staying

here for. So if you want me to stay, come here… *Now.*"

Pete listened until the big man started taking off Mother's clothes. He knew the big man was going to hurt Mother. He always got really scared when he hurt her like that. So he stopped listening and went to play fire-fighter.

Pete pushed the fire truck into the light and made the ladder go up to the window. He pretended the light was fire and the wooden frame was a giant house. He wanted to turn on the siren and lights and play like real firemen and fight the fire. But he was supposed to be sleeping and didn't want the big man to yell at him.

Fighting this fire was not easy. It took all of Pete's G.I. Joes to do it. Smiling, he took them down off the window ledge, one at a time, sliding them down the ladder to climb off the truck and stand together like real firemen do after they put out a big fire. He wished he could feed them sandwiches like people do on TV. He didn't have any sandwiches. Not even pretend ones.

Pete stood up quickly, excited. He knew where something even better than sandwiches was. It was in the kitchen.

Watermelon!

Pete smiled and walked to the door. He could give each of the firemen a piece of Mother's watermelon. And Mother would never know because the firemen were small. He could give them each a small piece.

He swiped a finger under his eye and peeked out into the hallway. It was quiet. But the hallway light was on so it wasn't scary quiet. He knew Mother was gone. Her car makes a lot of noise when it leaves the garage.

He walked into the living room. The big man was sleeping in Daddy's chair. Pete looked at the TV as he hurried past it. A cowboy movie was playing. There were horses running fast, and the men riding them had big funny hats and were shooting guns. Pete wanted to stop and watch the cowboys but he didn't want the big man to wake up and yell at him.

Walking into the kitchen Pete saw Mother's good knife on the counter. He slowly walked up to it. Reached up and touched the handle. Mother didn't want him playing with her good knife. She didn't want him even *touching* it. Or any knife.

He turned and looked at the big man. His eyes were closed. Pete grabbed the knife and looked at the blade. It was very shiny. He wondered if his firemen could use a good knife. Smiling, he swiped his eye, looked up at the refrigerator and remembered the watermelon.

The cold air pushed out against his face, blowing hair out of his eyes. It smelled like watermelon. Pete opened the refrigerator all the way and leaned in to look at the watermelon in Mother's big dish. She hadn't cut it up yet. He lifted the knife and pressed the blade into the green part people weren't supposed to eat. It didn't go in very far. He pulled it out and stuck it back in, harder this time. His hand slipped down the handle and scared him; he almost touched the blade.

Pete left the knife and walked away from the refrigerator. Then he stopped. His squinted eye stopped its rapid blinking. His panting slowed. He chewed on his lip. Then he went back to the watermelon and grabbed the knife with both hands. He jerked it clear and, without thinking, rammed it down hard into the melon. The handle thumped under his fingers, but didn't slip. He smiled and pulled the blade out slowly. Dark pink showed where the knife had been. Pete stared at the hole. Then he looked at the other end and pushed the knife in. Using both hands, he pretended they were paws and he was a giant bear. He pushed the knife in all over, making the green part have big holes that leaked pink water. Playing with Mother's good knife was really fun.

"What the hell?"

Pete gasped and spun away from the refrigerator. He put his hands behind his back.

"Who were you talking to? Aren't you supposed to be in bed? What the fuck time is it?" Eagle peered around the kitchen, wiping fingers over his eyes.

Pete stood, frozen, scared the big man was going to yell and call him stupid names.

Eagle smacked his lips and staggered towards the refrigerator. He stopped suddenly and looked down at Pete. He threw his hands out to his sides. "Well, you little fuck. Why are you just staring like a little pussy? Tell me who you were talking to. Fucking woke me up. You having a sleepover or some gay shit?" He glanced around, then leaned in and grabbed a beer, closed the refrigerator.

Pete shook his head. His eye watered. He wanted to wipe it. But he was scared he would hurt himself if he let go of Mother's good knife.

"Ah, you crying now little pussy? Did I hurt your little pussy feelings?" He took a big swallow of his beer. Sighed. His eyes narrowed. "Hey. You hiding something? What do you have behind your back?" He stepped toward Pete.

Pete held his breath. He gasped when the big man grabbed his shoulder and squeezed really hard.

"I asked you a goddamn question, boy. What's behind your back?"

The big man took hold of Pete's neck. His giant hand wrapped all the way around it, fingers touching thumb. He snatched Pete toward him.

Pete squeaked as he was yanked off the floor. The big man pulled him up so their faces almost touched. He tried to grab the big man's arm.

"I told you I will *not* be the head of a weak fam - " Eagle wasn't expecting the little pussy to hit him. And damn did it hurt! He dropped the boy and felt the side of his neck. His eyes widened. Beer sprayed from the can as it hit the floor. He started coughing and suddenly had trouble seeing. He felt sick, worse than any hangover. He felt for the counter and tried to move his feet over to the sink. But his feet wouldn't move. He opened his eyes wide and saw he was on his knees. He tried to resist coughing. It came out and the pain in his neck flared down his spine like a burn. It spread into his arms and legs, turning cold. Hot blood poured over trembling fingers. He gently touched the knife handle, thinking he would pull it out real quick. He grabbed the handle, eyes closed tight, groaning. Then lost his courage. He would wait for Bev. *She'll be home any minute...*

Pete watched the big man move around the kitchen. He moved like he does whenever he comes home from playing with his friends. It was funny. But it wasn't very funny this time. Mother was going to be really *really* mad about this mess.

The big man tried to pull Mother's good knife out of his neck. He couldn't. Pete walked over and took the handle in both hands, pulling it all the way out. It made a sucking sound. Pete froze, staring at the blade. Blood shot out of Eagle's neck and he screamed because it must hurt really bad. Pete felt blood running down his face. It felt gross but he kept looking at the knife.

Eagle clamped a hand over his neck and fell on his back. He coughed and pink spittle covered the cabinets he lay next to. His breaths were shallow. His eyes were locked onto Pete, on the knife the boy was staring at. Holding his eyes open made him want to puke. He was glad he didn't drink much today. The pain from puking right now would certainly kill him.

Pete's face turned toward the big man. Chewing on his lip, he held his hands out wide and waved the knife in front of him. He stomped over to Eagle. "You fucking my girl?"

Eagle jerked and blew out a high pitched wheeze. He screamed. His boots pushed at the cabinets, sliding him into the pink beer.

Pete jumped and landed on top of Eagle. He shouted in a deep voice, "Tell me how you did it!" and pushed the knife down into Eagle's chest. A boot caved in several cabinet doors, heel thudding on the tile.

Eagle pushed at the boy with all his strength but couldn't budge him. He tried to say "stop" but only coughed. His chest made him forget about his neck. He grabbed at the blade, cutting his fingers. Nausea swamped him. He groaned loud as the boy leaned back and slowly pulled it out. He managed one gasping breath before the knife plunged into the other side. He heard that deep voice say, "You're sorry? That's the same fucking thing she said. Sorry. You two were made for each other. Two sorry motherfuckers!" and then he heard no more.

***

Bev parked and got out. The garage door rumbled over her head, closed and locked. She walked around to the trunk and took out several bags of groceries. Closed it and walked inside the house.

She was dead tired. She hadn't slept much lately because of Pete's weird crap and Eagle's drunk bullshit. She nearly fell asleep during the long drive. *Almost died… Shit, I hope Eagle is sleeping.*

She hefted the bags and walked through the laundry room, into the kitchen. Groceries hit the floor, cans rolling into a pool of blood. On the other side Eagle lay against the counter cabinets. Bev screamed. Her eyes seized on Eagle's neck and chest and she kept on screaming.

Pete appeared from the living room. Bev jumped when she saw him. She started to run to him but saw the knife. She froze again.

His face…

"Expect? Hell if I know," the doctor had said, then laughed. "That's part of the fun."

Oh my fucking God.

Pete held his hands wide and waved the knife. He stomped over to her. "Fucking my girl?" He said in a thunderous voice. "Huh? DID YOU FUCK MY GIRL?"

Bev started screaming again.

Hunger

"**Y**ou're hurting me."

"Do not move."

Her thin arms bowed out, teeth bared as she held to the kitchen stool with all her might. "Stop it!" She began to slide off.

Tearing over the hallway carpet with its oversized paws, a German Shepherd puppy ran up behind the man and snapped at his leg. Jumped back, stumbling away from the huge boot casually swatted at his black muzzle.

"Ow! Let me go let me go!"

The man pushed harder. Pudgy fingers disappearing into the base of her neck.

Her bare feet kicked straight out, stool wobbling, heels rebounding off the floor. She clawed at his wrists, raking deep into his flesh with her short nails. The dog lunged in for another try.

The man let go. Leaned over and scratched behind the dog's ear.

Rebecca sprang forward, turned with a ripping curse distorting her freckled cheeks. Shoved golden scarlet locks behind her ears. Looked up. Her eyes, normally as large and mesmerizing as emeralds under water, were narrowed to slits.

"Better?" Paternal delight creased the man's weathered features. The dog looked back and forth between them, sitting, tongue lolling. It took all the fight out of her.

"Papa… Ugh-errr!" She huffed, still on her toes. Then the madness left. She laughed, rubbing the back of her neck. "The crick. How did you do that?"

"Thank you, Papa. I won't do gymnastics in the street again," he said in a little girl's voice. The dog stood and barked at him, pawed the floor. Looked at her.

"Thank you, Papa. And it wasn't gymnastics. It's called parkour."

He leaned down, grabbed her upper arms. The warmth and

power, the authority and security she experienced from her father's touch, made her grin up at him. He said, "No more parkour in the street. Understood?"

Her toes left the floor and she squeaked, laughing. "Okay okay! Put me down!" The dog darted back and forth, growling at him, stopped and licked her feet.

He pulled her into a hug, ignoring the sharp nips from her Shepherd. "Love you, Strawberry Fart."

"Love you, too, Stinky Ears." She squeaked again. "Now put me down!"

***

"Rebecca."

The house was missing it. The cozy fullness of a complete, happy family. The small brick home was tough to navigate with all the old furniture. At that moment, though, to her, it was a box of *loss.*

Rebecca looked up at her brother. Sammy resembled their dead father, tall and dark haired, shoulders that tested the seams of a wardrobe of denim work shirts. Her chin sank to her chest, breathless, trying hard not to cry again.

"I miss him. So much."

"Hey. Let's celebrate his life," Sammy said. "Not cry about it. Alright?"

She dabbed a tissue to her nose, the tip of it as reddened as the ends of her fingers. He sat next to her on the couch, followed her line of sight. Across the room the seat of the big recliner bore a deep impression, looked as if Papa had just stood from it. Maybe for a quick bathroom break or to grab another cup of coffee before the morning news came on.

Her cheek softened as she lay on his shoulder, and

the shiver about to pass through Sammy vanished.

The dog trotted in from the kitchen, paws ticking on the hardwood floor. Stopped in front of Rebecca and nuzzled her legs, long and very pale in bright yellow shorts. Looking up with a panting smile, bushy tail swaying, he closed his eyes when she rubbed between his ears.

"Hunger. Hey boy. There's a *good* boy!" she said. His tail smacked against the coffee table. "You hungry? Want something to eat?"

"Of course he's hungry." Sammy shifted on the couch, put his hand out. Hunger chuffed, closed his mouth. He backed away, tail straightened, eyes tracking the hand.

"He's just being a butt because I'm in the room. Soon as I leave he'll go back to begging for a scratch. Goofy eared mutt."

Sammy's forehead creased as he stood, Dockers bulging with fists pressed deep into them. "It's Saturday. You should take him out on the boat. You and Papa always go out on Saturday. You might feel better."

"Or worse." She hugged a pillow to her. "Always *went* out. It won't be the same." She looked at the recliner. Hunger barked, startling them both. Eyes meeting, they laughed.

"See? Hunger agrees with me. It's a good idea, right boy?"

Hunger looked at Rebecca, tip of his tongue flapping under a wet nose.

"What about funeral arrangements, and all his," she turned a palm up, *stuff?*

Keys clanged in Sammy's pocket. "Little sense in both of us going to the funeral home. Papa didn't want anything fancy, you know that."

"I can invite people."

"Like who? His friends from the shipyard? It's an

empty coffin. They've already seen the last of Papa - before the hull exploded." Angry now he moved around the dog, still watching him. "I'll take care of that. You need a breather before the wake tonight."

She reached for another tissue, arm brushing Hunger's flank. The box plopped back on the coffee table. "Well then I'll research how to do the account transfer. Sammy, there's too much to do."

From the other side of the table he tilted his head. "Honestly, are you in any shape to study banking right now?" He pointed his chin to the front of the house. Thumbs stuck out from his pockets. "Go on! Get outta here."

Rebecca beamed at her brother. Stood and motioned to Hunger.

Sammy caught her arm. "Eat something first. If Papa knew you were starving yourself again…"

Hands moving to cover her jutting hip bones, hair fell loose from one ear. "Papa knew. I'll take something with me." One side of her mouth turned up. Snatching up a pillow, she hit him with it. "If he knew you were still taking Molly…"

Pulling on his bottom lip, blinking, he looked at her and couldn't keep embarrassment from shading his face.

Her laughter rang out. A moment passed and he joined her.

Hunger's ears lay back. He took a step toward Sammy and barked.

***

The 90 horsepower Johnson only needed half throttle to make the boat skip over the small waves. The aluminium pontoons resonated with sharp booms, salty spray arching up and away from the sides. The roar of the motor buzzed, her arms from gripping the wheel. Her hair, strawberry blonde in the morning sun, whiplashed behind a face warped by the cutting punch of speeding into the warm wind.

Hunger stood at the bow with his paws wide, long black hair streaked with color from the slanting sun. It was his third time out. Rebecca no longer worried every time he lost balance from the boat planing over a particularly tall wave. Scrambling for purchase, he always righted himself with a series of wild barks. Rebecca, grinning over the center mounted console, barked with him.

Navigation had been her father's part of the outings. She, the pilot, with his voice shouting over the wind, guiding her speed and direction, she never lost her way. The endless waves racing past, the glowing, beckoning horizon, were her only awareness.

She looked from the expanse of dawn to the front of the boat. Hunger faced her, his familiar whine piercing, then he turned and barked at the water.

She grabbed the throttle, pulled it back. "What's the matter?"

He whined, set his paws wide as the boat slowed and ramped up and down. The fast flow of wind buzzed her barren of feeling. Sensation slowly returned, the boat crawling up and over choppy seas.

It was hot for September. She could anchor and swim to the island. Walk the shore barefoot and add to her shell collection, take some pictures. She tensed at the thought. Then, "Idiot. I forgot my camera." She stood from looking under the console. "Hunger, I'm sorry boy. I didn't bring us anything to eat either."

His head dipped low, whites of eyes pink as the

sun rose to their left. His tongued his nose, grumbled a whine. He wagged his tail.

"Idiot. I know. I already said it. You don't always have to agree with me, you know. I'll still feed you and pet you."

A huge wave banged into the side of the boat. Rebecca caught herself on the wheel, laughing at Hunger's antics. The exhaust of the idling motor sputtered above the waterline, quieted below. "Let's just swim to the island and walk the beach. Sound good to you?"

Hunger stood, tail swishing. His tongue extended, his eyes on her.

She pointed a finger. "No chasing seagulls. *No.*"

His eyes closed. Mouth opened wider.

Slipping out of her flip flops, she leaned in front of the console and picked up the anchor. Looked to the right. Hunger whined as she spun around and dropped it. The steel struck the deck with a dull thud.

"The island. Hunger... *Holy shit.*"

She sat behind the wheel and found herself staring at the seat next to her, it's deep impression. Sliding into it she looked around. Light headed, her pulse beat against the arm of the chair from her wrist. Chopping waves struck the pontoon she was looking over, spray misting her arms and hair. Hunger whined and clawed his way over the titling deck, in between the seats. His wet nose snuffled her leg, pushed up her shorts.

"We can't be... I'm not sure..." Her ponytail swung left, right. She pointed at the horizon, finger bathed with green cutting through yellow, sky hinting at blue. "If that's east, then the island is... We came from the *north.*" Hair pulled loose from the tie, slim fingers sinking into it. Standing, she turned in a slow circle. There was no land in site.

Hunger whined, lay at her feet.

"We're not screwed just yet, boy."

He licked her toes.

"We just head north. Right? Can't be hard to find. Keep the sun on the right," she pointed at it, her other finger aimed straight ahead, "and go that way."

Her toes clenched the deck, vibration from the spitting engine giving her a start. The engine died.

Hunger, paws wide, looked up at her. His tongue snapped into his mouth.

She looked from the fuel gauge. "Okay. Now we're screwed completely."

***

Without flippers she had to rely on her arms. She was surprised at how much stronger she felt in the water, pleased about all the parkour practice, thinking of the unexpected benefits. Rebecca would tire, but she knew how to pace herself, recover, and keep going.

The noon sun pinked the tops of her ears, cheeks beginning to color the same. Slipping below a wave she adjusted the anchor-line on her waist and decided to swim a little further.

Hunger, at his place on the bow, panting, watched her. A salty breeze pushed his ears forward. Several times he ran to the stern barking. Rebecca heard small splashes and smiled. Then recalled something her father once said.

"You see those fish?"

She followed his finger, held a hand to her eyes. "Is that a school of mullet?" A dozen or more of them were launching out of the waves.

"No. Not this far out. Those are mackerel. With something big after them."

With something big after them.

Her legs drifted down, arms treading fast in between the boat and a small wave extending out before her. Mindful of her breathing she kept the water from sucking in. It took a moment to push through the gelatinous nature her body had become; she suddenly *knew* something big was after her.

Head dipped under, whirling to face the boat, she grabbed the line and yanked herself in that direction. She kicked out hard, shoulders bobbing above the surface. Hunger barked, muzzle hanging over the side, tail high behind him. His swaying shadow dispersed into the water's reflection on the aluminium pontoon. The glow dimmed entirely as her knees scrubbed onto the outdoor carpet. Hunger's wet nose hit hers and she let out a shout, the deck rising to meet her elbows. She twisted around and hugged the dog to her. Heads hung over the water, her hair and his blew into her eyes.

A gray blur under the waves sped off, its path traced by geysers of white branching in all directions, massive school of fish launching into beaming daylight to escape the murderous predator.

Her hug tightened. He licked her shoulder.

***

Torn. That's how her throat felt. Shallow, labored pants scraping, slicing over her swollen tongue. Hunger swayed into her, claws digging for purchase next to her thigh. They looked at each other. She put her forehead to his nose and felt the fever in it. She blocked his lick before it burned across her face. His breaths were louder, dryer, as they passed into the third day.

Hunger's tail swept up as he turned. She ducked

away and the skin on her shoulders stretched. The pain snarled her blistered face. Lips sucked in she made her eyes relax and allowed a little air in through her nose. The shadow the shorts on her head made, grew larger as she sank down, legs hanging next to the cool pontoon in shadow.

There was no canopy, nothing to use to cover herself. A search for towels ended with Rebecca in her underwear and a shorts sombrero on her head.

Which is more uncomfortable? She examined the tip of her finger, red with blood from her bottom lip. *The dry-then-sticky pink fire of serious sunburn, or your gut rebelling against foreign microbes?*

She brushed the half eaten jellyfish from her lap into a glimmering wave that wet her toes. It was the only thing she could catch for them to eat, using her shirt as a net, on shark duty because the only place with shade was hanging off the side of the boat.

Hunger wouldn't even sniff the slimy creature plopped in front of him. She told herself survival depended on her having energy, a silent mantra that assisted her in choking it down. More than once she looked to the clouds and promised her father she would never starve herself again. The courageous intentions stopped four bites later.

***

Rebecca quivered with fatigue. The act of dying corkscrewed into ideas, the process of death tweaked clenched eyelids. Mortality, a keen interest for the first time in her nineteen years.

It has to be better...

The empty motor oil can was slick in her feeble grasp. The knots in her stomach, winching tight, rebelled her attempts to reach down to the water. The pontoons tucked into the oncoming whitecaps, twin gray spears she envisioned ripping through her, slick mound of intestines as pink as her flesh.

I must be dying. Her vision sharpened for a moment. *Please let me be dying!*

She raised the can and sipped. The taste of oil was strong, but it was the saltwater her body refused to keep down. Purging the jellyfish was the original idea, then hydration; she hoped it would ease the distress biting deep within her poisoned innards. Just slipping over the side and soaking in the cool blue drink was inviting. *The relief... shit!* The hard expression she directed at the water - the sea she once loved - broke with a sob. The can dropped. She clutched herself, drew in her elbows.

Noticing the console was dark on the stern side now she wondered how long she had been out. Between vomiting and uncontrollable diarrhoea she could only doze. Hunger lay next to her, his tail on her neck, shivering. *Is he alright?*

The dog shifted and began to lap away at the light brown fluid coating her thighs. He pushed his muzzle into her buttocks.

Hunger! That's... no!

He gave a low whimper but didn't stop, ducking away from her attempt. The dog she loved, *knew*, wasn't the one going at her with blind desperation. The terror held sadness, hitting at once.

She couldn't stop him.

The shade... Just on the other side of the console.

Shoving away from Hunger required something essential that was vacant in her: the ability to get up. Line of sight flat on the deck, the inflammation pulsing on her limbs knew the carpet fibers to be lethal.

"Simple enough," she whispered, visualizing maneuvers to get to the sunless haven beneath the wheel. At that moment it was parkour in the extreme. "Nope."

Pulling the shorts from her head she took a fillet knife from a pocket. Papa's spare. It was the only thing that turned up during the hunt for fishing tackle. He never kept his good Mercer on board since the fish finder disappeared the day after they got the boat.

Rebecca held the sheath and thought back to their first boat ride. A memory she compared to every fishing trip and island cruise since.

"Did you get high?" her brother said that evening on the back porch, helping her clean the fish. "You doing Molly?"

"No, dork." Glancing into the house she lowered her voice. "But if it's as fun as we had today I see why you do. Best day *ever.*"

"I thought you said the ferry ride to the island was the best ever."

"That was forever ago."

"Uh-huh."

"Why did you ask if I was high? Do I look high?"

Sammy looked up. "Yes. And because you were begging Papa to let you sleep on the boat!"

"I know, yeah." Head tilted down with a smile. "So we wouldn't have to leave from the house - "

"We would already be on the boat," Papa said. "That was the most charming and by far the silliest thing to ever come out of your pretty little head."

She could still see him, filling the kitchen door, holding the book bag she packed for the night: snacks, cards, and a magazine. She wanted to finish reading about reindeer in Russia for a school assignment. He had taken it - and her - from the boat earlier.

She shrugged. Her brother grabbed another fish and took a knife to it. It was clean of scales in record time.

"Don't worry. I didn't hear you talking about Molly." His face appeared to be painted a dull iron next to the light burning above the door, eyes polished gold. His sleeve slid down as he pointed. "Come on Strawberry. You really want to camp on that hard thing? Let's hear a better reason."

"Um…" She pushed up on her toes. "So no one will steal it. I'll be a guard."

Papa laughed. "You would make a terrifying guard, for sure. But if those thieves wanted the boat they would have taken it, not just the fish finder."

"Oh."

He tossed the bag to her. "Okay. I'm convinced. I'll get my bag and camp with you."

She felt excitement shining from her eyes but still managed to look serious. "Guard. We aren't camping."

"Sorry. I'll guard the boat with you. Let me get a bag and I'll meet you out front." He went inside, stuck his head back out. "Sammy. Molly better be a real girl. If she's not, don't wait too long before you break up. Girls like that make you forget things. Like plans for college. Or two plus two."

"Huh?"

"Yes sir, is what you meant to say."

"Yes sir!"

The boat smelled awful that night, her and Papa talking and watching the stars. Laughing when a neighborhood mutt tore through Mr. Davis' trash…

The elation was gone now. Rebecca hated that night. Wished the boat had been taken. Fishing, exploring the islands and camping near the shores - she hated all of it.

It's too hot! Everything burns…

I hate you, Papa!

Neck limp, her skull bounced once. Clouds rushed down from above, weight building, closing her off from the horror that became of this trip.

Deep gasp... And the chill of the Russian arctic seeped into her joints, the stench of rotting tundra on her reindeer skin boots and gloves.

Her muscles burned. The Nenets were making the eight hundred mile migration to reach summer pastures in the North. The elders spoke of the years ahead as ones of adapting, to a new world of animals breeding too soon and the snows coming and going at times that would make farming a losing gamble. Gas lines will cross fields the Nenets used for grazing since time before the tales of their ancestors. The screaming roar of jets from airports, cell towers and Internet service. The boarding schools their children went to would teach science in place of their religion.

Rebecca told herself to worry about the problems of the day. *No sense getting scared about problems that weren't problems quite yet.*

"Do you miss the Kara Sea?" the herder said in greeting. Tawny skins flared out from his short frame, leading a trio of reindeer in the tall grass beyond the path. Harnesses strapped on their stout barrel necks, the strays were the source of reproof looking at her from within the hood of his jacket. "They run off, but a handful of moss turns them into puppies that won't stop following you."

"That one needs watching," Rebecca said, looking from the moss held in his glove to the reindeer in front.

The fearless deserter bobbed her head, nose pointing. Stepped up to the man and chomped at the gray tufts of lichen.

"Haha, too late!"

"She's a rascal, yeah?" The others weren't to be left out, nudging ahead, velvet antlers colliding. "Alright, ladies! Wait your turn!"

"Have fun with that."

His dark oiled hood ducked in her direction. Lifting the traces the herder moved on, outpacing Rebecca and the group of women steering sleds at the rear of the caravan.

"Nenets haven't been to the Kara Sea since the rain on snow." The woman had to look up at Rebecca, a tired sideways glance. "Four summers since our herds were cursed."

Rain on snow? Rebecca tugged on her lip. Then she recalled the man from the government, the explanation of the event four years past.

Mass graves of reindeer buried in the 1940s anthrax outbreak had made it back to the surface. The bacteria survived the slow thawing ascent to once more bring death to life. The government contained it, though not before it destroyed the herds and changed the Nenet way for good. It could happen again, everyone knew.

"We could use some snow," Rebecca said, failing to think of a new topic. Disaster was everywhere, on every face, in every thought. The skids on the heavily laden sleds dragged, scraped at the dry ground. With no snow or ice the burden on the reindeer pulling the sleds added to the imminent demise of the 30,000 Nenets on the Yamal Peninsula.

"We are stronger and wiser than any rain on snow."

Rebecca eased her grip on the traces, reindeer snorting, stomping behind her. The woman spoke true. Their people had thrived in the arctic region for centuries. Through Russian oppression the Nenet way lived on.

We must adapt or perish.

"We will take this path to the sea and our herds will provide," she said. The woman bent low and urged the two bulls powering her sled up a slope.

Rebecca gripped and pulled, looked back at the beasts and whistled. Streams of breath plumed, obscuring their dark snouts. *When will the caravan make camp?*

The baby on her back shrieked. Rebecca let go of the traces. Two girls ran up to loosen the harness on her back and talk sweetly to the hungry infant. Gloves hanging from leather thongs on her wrists, Rebecca held Vera to her exposed breast and covered them both with a hide blanket. The stench of it made her gag.

The wailing child stirred the mothers trekking the sad field. The girls ran off when the older women shouted at the herders. The men shouted in response, whistles spread through the caravan, which slowed and stopped.

Vera was getting heavier every month, except for this one. Rebecca vowed to eat more and wished she had during the pregnancy. She hated to deceive Pedava, but her husband had his duties and didn't need to hear that his baby may not live to play on the shore of the Kara.

Pushing back her hood she scanned the slope of matted grass. Reindeer in the hundreds were marching upwards, vanishing on the plain.

The grinding sleds silent, she hummed to Vera and sought comfort amid the snorts and pawing of the resting pack animals. Her beloved pets. A herder spoke as he approached, massive boots layered with pelts whispering over the tundra. "Pedava sent me. His tent will be full tonight."

"Why? Did someone get hurt?"

A small sled heaped with fresh kills crept by, a single bull lead by a herder in modern camouflage. They watched it go by and grinned at one another. He said, "He is slow. If the meat is cold, you women will want to eat *him.*" He flicked his lasso as if to toss it. "I will help him."

"We are right behind you."

Her husband's tent was indeed packed. Men with black hair and women with serious expressions sat with children around the edges. Hanging behind them were large handmade rugs with elaborate patterns of gold and red over darker bases. Some of her tribe going in and out holding portions of meat wore clothes made of the same material. Most were eating quietly, bundled in their skins.

Rebecca pushed in and crouched, hefting the baby above two butchered reindeer. Her mouth watered, fingers digging out her knife. A woman older than the tundra reached over the crude, pungent spread and took Vera.

Familiarity guided Rebecca's touch, stroking the hair, smelling it. Her hand clamped onto a fold of flesh with a reptilian twitch. The thin blade vanished and reappeared. Rivulets of hot nutrients coated her fingers, cached between knuckles. She immediately sucked at them.

She ate the first piece fast. The flesh warmed her frosted lips, the juices heated her carnivorous intent. The bull must have ran far after the shot, pumped full of adrenaline. Her jaw ached, so she swallowed the tough meat without chewing.

The tarp under the feast held pools of watery gore. Rebecca dropped to her knees in it and drove the knife in, pulled and sliced, freeing a much larger section that she would eat on the path.

Wiping eyes and cheeks she thought about returning after the tent cleared. The children collected the useful bones and remains. She pressed a hand to her belly. She would seduce Padava on this very spot...

***

"Strawberry! Whoa, hey… What the blazes!"

His voice pulled her up, twisting out of the spiral. The transition between worlds, imagined and real, was humbling, consciousness and soul merging into fresh awareness. A universal secret had been revealed, and demanded its price in pain.

"Let me go!"

The man released his hold and stepped back, visibly shaken by her gasp of torment. A length of intestines squished under his bare foot. "Ho damn, what! My eyes, Strawberry. Can you tell me what happened? Who did this?"

Rebecca lay on her side and stared up at her Papa. Her lips puckered. "You died. Then I died?"

His face, thinner than she remembered, wrinkled as he looked around the boat. "You didn't die. Me? I was always a deadbeat, right?"

His chuckle trailed off. He cupped a hand to the scruff on his jaw, watching his daughter struggle to make sense of it before losing consciousness again.

***

Each rushing wave pushed in, collapsed, sucking away sediment left by the high tide. The gentle lapping would make her sleepy, her Papa knew, and used to tell her stories of enormous dolphins that conducted the smaller dolphins in a swimming orchestra, singing and dancing that made the waves *just right for little strawberry haired girls that didn't want to go to sleep*. His laugh swelled inside the tent.

"That doesn't work anymore, Papa."

"Whoa, well look at that. She's still a little

sasshole. Good for you." His searching look fixed on her face. "I'll have to send a request to the conductor for an encore." Placing an air violin under his chin he hummed, elbow high on his sawing arm.

Rebecca watched the image of her Papa, making sure not to blink. She raised her chin, trembling. Forced to swallow, her eyes shut tight. The outline of ghost Papa followed her into darkness.

Jellyfish, oil in the sea water, the memory of the taste made her throat constrict. Ice touched her forehead and she knew this was real. She could see and hear, smell the sea, all at once. Every part of her burned, sweated. "Take the blanket away." She sat up. "Where's Hunger?"

He turned, set the Ziploc of ice and the blanket at her feet. Her head shifted to see past him. A fast moving blot of gray soared over the bright sand outside the tent, seagull coming into view, diving behind cresting waves.

Knowing Hunger's shadow wouldn't be trailing the bird, wouldn't be wagging into the tent with his wet legs and belly to lick her feet and beg for food, hurt swelled in Rebecca.

Sweat beaded on her shoulder, though it was cold, the warmth of her companion missing; Hunger would have been at her side, panting tongue ready to greet her as soon as she woke.

If he was alive.

The hurt intensified. A red vision spiked with the panic: Papa lifting her from the boat, his wide, dark feet moving carefully over glossy splashes of blood next to…

Her tongue pushed loose a stringy piece of meat and she screamed.

"Ah, Strawberry. You don't remember what happened?" He saw her pupils dilate, her hands curl into fists, and he bent down to grab her.

"It was you! YOUR FAULT!"

He winced, her foot smacking into his chest. Pinning her arms, he pressed his weight over her. "Now hold on. You - the boat was supposed to have just enough fuel to get you to the island. We didn't know you would get lost! I'm in debt with some bad people. The insurance... Just let me - how in blazes did you miss the island, Strawberry?"

"You killed my fucking dog!"

"No, I don't know how... Come on, you know we all loved Hunger. What are you saying? Let me explain!"

"Your fault! YOUR FUCKING FAULT, PAPA!"

"What are you doing? You need to rest while I think this over. We can't tell anybody." He pushed down. *"You can't tell anybody."*

Her legs bunched. "You need to FUCKING LET ME GO."

Rocking back on her shoulders, Rebecca kicked both feet into his face. His teeth snapped, neck and shoulders lengthened, but his grip remained, tips of his strong fingers paralyzing the nerves in her wrists.

"Stop! Just stop!"

"Fuck you!"

He pushed forward, her legs over his shoulders. She planted a heel in his eye socket and twisted at the waist, immediately throwing herself back the other way, striking the tent's center brace. Nylon came down on them.

The sand beneath the tent floor was cool on her knees, heated where her hands dug into it outside. Snaking loose from a grasp on her leg Rebecca slipped out and stumbled upright, swaying, hand held in front of her. Papa's shouts were muted, the breaking waves silent. She willed herself to stay on her feet, blinking at the sun.

Her chest had never hurt so much. Her stomach

roiled with stress.

Where are you, boy? You're such a good boy! Hunger! Where are you? You goofy eared mutt.

Seagulls glided past, beaks pointed at the surf. She turned with a smile, watching Hunger dart from behind a sand bank, where he was poorly hidden, tail twitching in a thicket of reeds. The seagulls must have thought his bark was hysterical, giving notice with caws that sounded like peals of laughter. Rebecca's abs cramped as she joined them.

Why is it so hot?

Hunger ran towards her, tongue flapping from the side of his grin. A shell bit into her foot, deep in the sand preventing her from following the dog. Hunger ran past. Her face throbbed, going numb as sound vanished once more. Head turned to track the blurring animal...

The reindeer was down, though it wasn't dead, hooves struggling to find purchase in the tundra. *Where is the herder?* She searched the horizon, knowing he must be close. She bit her lip.

She couldn't wait, couldn't take the chance of the bull escaping.

She felt around her waist, looked up. Her knife was on the ground behind the animal. She ran to it.

Dropping the sheath she crouched with the blade in front and advanced. The reindeer reared and pawed the air with a terrible cry that made her face ache. She screamed back and lunged in. The thin steel ripped in at his gut and came out below his chest. A hoof struck her, the bull toppled forward. The tundra cushioned the weight of the enormous beast that slammed her down.

Thick coarse hair on the bull's neck smashed against her panting lips. A flood of hot blood soaked her and she gave a winning growl, jabbing her blade into the neck. Wet snorts softened and slowed, movement ceased to a dead weight.

Padava will be so happy!

Freeing herself from the kill, she knelt and cut a huge chunk from the leg, licked at the juices and took a bite. "Our people will survive, Vera," she told the baby harnessed on her back. She rubbed a fold of skin between thumb and finger, decided it would make a good bed roll. She shushed the crying child. "We are stronger and wiser than any rain on snow."

Libby's Hands

"**I** hid her from everyone."

Dina squeezed the old woman's hand. Her mouth widened, corners perked up. She glanced around the room and leaned over the bed, whispered, "Where did you hide it, Grandma?"

"Not it. Her. I hid *her* from everyone. You think I'm addled." She moved her hand away, rubbed it with the other. Dark purple veins looped over tendons pushing up through paper thin wrinkles.

Dina sat looking at her grandmother's sagging face, recalling the vitality it had just last holiday season.

"How is she?" Dina's mother said from the door. She folded her arms, started to lean on the frame. Glanced over a shoulder and leapt into the room, a cluster of nurses and a cart rolling by.

Dina looked up from Grandma Catrick's withered hands to her mother. Tracie was short with eyes that matched her dark brown hair. *I'll go from this to that to...* She sucked in her lips, watching her grandma's bulbous nose flare; she had nodded off.

Tracie walked to the bed, one high heel in front of the other, purse in hand. Smoothing her long white skirt she sat in the chair next to the headboard and put a hand to her mother's forehead. "She was out of her mind earlier. Tell me she's done talking about wedding cake and yard tools."

Bright beams of sunlight poured into the room from the tall window behind Dina, her hair absorbing it in a halo effect, face cut with shadows. She turned and squinted at the panes, rattling from a sharp gust. "She was saying something like, 'I hid her from everyone'." She faced her mom, stole the purse from her lap and fished out a pack of gum. Unwrapped a stick.

"Jesus fucking Christ." Tracie yanked her purse back, crossed her legs. "That again."

"Again?"

"Your aunt Macie had a kid when she was your age. Mom put her up for adoption."

"No way... In, like, what? The '20s?"

Tracie held her purse up to throw it. "You and fucking old people jokes." She swatted the air in front of her daughter's smirk. "Late '70s. Teen pregnancies back then, God, *fuck,* you'd think the poor girls were Satan incarnate the way everyone acted."

"It's kinda still like that, mom."

She nodded. "Well, that's true, huh? But deformities were still seen as signs of evil and wrongdoing. Curses, and all that bullshit. Now deformed children are loved. Special little motherfuckers."

"And bullied."

"You know what I mean. Loved by their parents. No one is publicly shunning their kid because they're fucked up. If anything the fucked up kids get more love and attention."

"Until they go to school."

"Uh-huh. Well, I have to go." Tracie stood and bent at the waist, swished hair out of her way and kissed her mother's cheek. Looked at Dina. "Don't forget I need your help with decorations."

"Jack 'o lanterns, scary music, and hand out the bowls of candy. Got it."

"Don't look like that."

"You are going out." Her nose tilted. "You expect me to get dressed up, do all the decorating and shit, for a bunch of whiny, spoiled nose miners in princess outfits?"

"Yes. And they're adorable. Take some pictures for me."

"Sure. Then you'll get to see their ruined makeup, after the boys too old for trick-or-treating steal their candy and show up at our door with their Halloweenies."

Tracie clucked her tongue, shouldered her purse and rolled her eyes.

"So... wait." Dina inspected her nails. "So, there's like... I have a cousin out there somewhere. And they're deformed?"

"Yes. Maybe. Shit, who knows? She may be dead."

"She. It was a girl with... What? What kind of deformity?"

"I don't know, Dina. A bad one is all I know."

"She's the Devil bad?" She looked up and grinned.

Tracie laughed. "I guess so. Oh," her eyebrows arched, "your uncle will be there."

"Well yeah, I figured that."

"Be nice."

"Aren't I always?"

"Nope." She waved to a person in the hall on the way out.

Dina took the gum from her mouth and threw it after her. Then yelped, a cold hand clamping down on her wrist.

"I hid her from everyone. Your mother... I tried. She wouldn't believe me."

"You were awake? You scared the *shit* out of me." Her chest knocked, face drained of color.

Grandma Catrick's voice, dry and cracking with high tones, rose clear and sturdy, the matriarch of old. "Dina, listen to me. You have to decorate the tree by the pond. The hands, you see. They must be perfect." Her grip tightened. She lifted her head. Bags puffed out beneath her eyes.

Dina patted the hand locked on her arm. Concern

softened her words. "Grandma… Alright. I'll put some hands on the tree. Just like you used to."

"Not just any hands. Perfect ones. Life-like." She squeezed. Lay down again. "Like yours. Or Libby, she'll… You must promise me."

The imploring drained the authority from her voice, the strength from her grip. A moan escaped from under an arm raised to shield her weeping face.

Dina's felt her pulse on her breaths. *Okay, I'm seriously done here.* Licking her lips, she wiped damp palms on her jeans and darted from the chair. Bumped into a shelf. A figurine crashed to the floor. Dina stepped back and crunched down on it. She looked down and saw porcelain fingers sticking out from beneath her boot.

Shaking off an ill trance she rushed out of the nursing home.

***

"Help! I'm bleeding to death! Please help me! I'm serious! I'm bleeding to death! Help!"

Dina grinned at her Uncle Taylor, moved in front of him and turned the volume down. Pulling on his mustache, Taylor watched the light bars on the stereo equalizer, blinking as the recording pleaded for help.

"Sounds real, huh? Like there's really someone in Grandma's garage bleeding to death."

He waited for her to finish speaking, started pulling at his mustache again.

Frightened, squealing and laughing children turned into the long, curving driveway. Dina picked up a bowl of candy and shook it. "Coming?" she said walking around the table and chairs set up in front of the garage.

Taylor's stomach rose and fell. He turned without

a word and retrieved his candy bowl, followed his niece past rows of glowing pumpkins to meet the group.

"I saw these tiny packages of salad and almost got a cart full to hand out with the junk," Dina said to a lady with a green face in a black witch outfit, handing Butterfingers to the kids in front of her.

A three foot Sponge Bob accepted it with his head down, a scrape of his toe on the concrete. The other kid, a boy dressed as a blue cupcake with a matching blue handlebar mustache, snatched the candy bar from her hand with a triumphant growl. He tore it open and stuffed the entire thing in his mouth. He stepped forward and stuck his hand in the bowl.

"Adam! *No.* My goodness, I'm sorry," the witch said, black nails clinging to the boy's cupcake. "Maybe a Fun Size Salad is what he needs."

"No salad!" Adam growled and swatted at the bowl.

Dina held the bowl up and stuck her tongue out. "I knew it would be a tough sell."

"It would be the end of trick-or-treating as we know it. You want to ruin Halloween, Adam?"

"No salad!"

They laughed. Dina said, "I think you're right, dude. The candy corporations wouldn't allow it, anyway. Probably buy the salad company just to stop it."

Sponge Bob turned back and forth, watching the adults. Taylor leaned away from the kids, still pulling on his mustache.

A larger group approached. A wizard and elf towering over a handful of goblins. The witch's green face turned to Dina and rolled her eyes when she saw who the wizard was. Dina gave her a questioning look. The witch shrugged, *Good luck with that,* and shooed her kids down the drive.

"How many do we get?" the wizard said. He took the Butterfinger from Dina. Then helped himself to Taylor's bowl of Snickers.

Dina shook her head. *They* get one each. Put those back, please. Here you go." She pasted on a sweet smile for the goblins. A little girl with orange striped pigtails had trouble keeping her mask straight while holding up her bag. She pulled at the rubber mask and bumped into the elf behind her. Dropped her bag. Candy scattered.

"Look at the little dummy. Haha!" The wizard pointed. The other goblins laughed with him.

"Don't be an asshole, Ryan." The elf took ear buds from her huge ears and picked up the mess. The little girl stood crying, tiny hands wringing the mask

Dina took a picture, pocketed her phone, smiling. The wizard stared at her. She ignored him and told the elf, "Okay, this one gets two. Because she's so adorable." She motioned for Taylor to give the distraught goblin a Snickers.

***

She wasn't going to read the text. Then ringtones sounded from the elf and wizard. The stirrings of doubt made Dina pull the phone from her back pocket.

"It's an Amber Alert." The elf's nose was visible through the fake one attached over it, bright screen of her enormous phone exposing it. "A 12 year old boy and a 14 year old girl. From… *That's my street!*"

The goblins stopped moving their plastic bags, costumes freezing. A few houses down a phone rang, people walking out into the street, shouting for kids to go home.

"I knew I heard sirens," the wizard said. He unwrapped a Snickers. "Wonder who it is. I hope it's your neighbors. The ones that always leave their bikes in the street? I hate them."

"Unbelievable right now, Ryan."

"Couldn't have been you. Fucktard. *Leave.*" Dina took a step toward him without thinking, phone drawn back to strike. "There's about to be another alert."

"Let's go. I can't believe you said that." The elf huddled the goblins and shot an apologetic glance over her shoulder. The wizard flicked his wrapper at Taylor and followed, dropping his head as he passed Dina's glower.

Dina couldn't relax, pinched the bridge of her nose, "I wanted Halloween to end quickly. Not like this, though." She bumped her uncle's elbow with the bowl. "Uncle Taylor?"

His back to her, he yanked on his mustache and watched the stereo lights jump.

"Help! I'm bleeding to death! Help me... *please.* I'm bleeding to death!"

***

She knew. Somehow she knew it was connected.

She ran. Light from the back porch glistened on the wet grass, shoes soaked by the time she reached the pond. The tree was on the other side. A huge sycamore with low hanging branches, thick black tangled mass with the moon behind it.

"*Ah!*" Dina slipped on the path next to the water, nearly splashing in. Dirt on her hands, grass on her knees, wrinkled her nose.

Shoving to her feet she marched along the path, wary of the waterline and the tall grass she knew harbored snakes. Patterns of small branches ran over her, growing larger as she drew nearer the sycamore. Shrouded in total darkness at its base.

I promised. And forgot.

Fucktard!

The hand figurines hit against her leg. She rolled the Walgreens bag tight and stepped over the roots, hand sliding over the bark of the trunk. The icky tickle of a spider web stretched over her face and she squeaked and fell, ankle catching it bad between roots. The base of the sycamore met her lower back with a protruding knot. She hit and jerked away, sucking in a breath.

"Oh-wow-fuck… *fuck fuck fuck.*"

The shock to her spine stole the mobility of her legs, heels of her boots sliding over the ground without purchase. Moving off the knot she lay there holding in a scream. Not from the pain flaring from her ankle or the bruise spreading from her spine. Her new phone was crushed.

"$500 piece of trash." She smushed her lips between thumb and fingers. She had never been so mad at herself. Pulling the device from her pocket took effort. Her fingers traced over the busted case. As she held it close to her face the screen came on, full brightness, a kaleidoscope of colors swirling out from the point of impact. "$500 fucktard flashlight." She shined it around where she sat.

Dead leaves covered hard dirt. A few feet away the leaves were dark. She swept the light as far as she could in both directions. Back to the dark spot. Pushed to her feet, a tentative step, found her confidence and walked over to investigate.

What is that… wet something.

Large dry leaves crunched, silencing crickets, a breeze cutting through it, shaking the branches overhead.

She started to squat and lower the light.

Deep in the woods behind the sycamore, a scream started. High, shrill, the fear in it put an acidic taste in Dina's mouth, the tortuous shriek it transitioned to turning her spine to water. She pressed the phone to her stomach. Strained to see the line of trees across the tall grass. "I knew it. Oh goddamn I'm too late."

Blinking, fumbling the phone, she wiped her eyes and shined the light on her arm. A scattering of thick red drops ran across her forearm and up her sleeve.

It's in my eyes!

Turning, disoriented. Branches under strain of the wind lashed her with leaves. Bringing the phone up as a shield, Dina rocked back from a heavy limb. She thought her heart would explode when the light showed it to be two bloody stumps of hands whipping down at her.

Teeth cutting into her lip couldn't stop her mouth from stretching wide. Her scream tore through the distance, wavering, tears welling with a gasp to renew it.

A sharp blow to her skull silenced the fear.

***

It was the face of a boy. Much younger than her.

Why is he scared?

"What's wrong?" she said, though couldn't hear her words. A moment later she knew his terror as her own. She remembered.

She couldn't move. Hands tied together on the other side of a small tree. Head strapped to it, cheekbone sticking to pine bark. Less than a foot away the boy faced her, similarly bound, arms pulled tight around a small pine. His hands were out of sight.

She knew they were in the woods. It was too dark

to tell much else. The wind was picking up, a sea of mist passing above the treetops blending into elongating clouds. Both of Dina's ears hurt. Excruciating pain. Her left from her head pressed against the bark. Her right... Someone hit her, she knew. It had a pulse, her head swam with it. Bruised stiff, her back spasmed, her legs shook as she tried to stand and ease the tension. The bark ripped at the flesh around her eye. She pushed up on calves that burned with cold trembles. The back of her throat felt gashed, dry breaths coming fast. She felt herself losing consciousness, fighting it.

Spit hit her and she flinched awake, the boy's shout warm then cool, saliva continuing to coat her eyes. Through the deafness she felt his roaring gasps. A wrenching twist of cartilage popped through the tree trunk and she spat vomit.

A dim smear of moon shined on the boy. Teeth bared, his neck ballooned out from beneath an old strip of linen. The rest of him was a tense darkness in her peripheral.

A wet tearing and his mouth went slack, full body spasms scraping his binds over the hard bark. The sight of his face, the sound of his death throws... The intimate experience of murder shredded what little hold she retained of hope.

The boy's arms fell loose and his head slipped the loop. Dead weight bumped the ground. Dina strained to see his hands. The one by his side was wound in cloth. The other... was missing. Pine straw absorbed the remainder of his life, a trail oozing from the stump as his convulsing body was dragged out of her line of sight.

The woman walked in a crouch, a strange give to her knees that compressed the twigs and pine cones under foot without breaking them. Dina's cheek opened up, cloth holding her head resisting her effort to see.

The woman held a stick, stabbing it at something in her armpit. Dark ratty hair fell to below her breasts, shifting in a flannel shirt she wore like an apron.

"Libby."

Dina's cousin gave a terrible screech and darted over the straw. The end of the stick jabbed into her shoulder. Dina lost her next words, screaming, spittle ejected before her lips snapped closed. Libby struck again. Snatched it loose and took aim.

The boy's hand hit the ground and picked up leaves rolling between her feet. Dina saw it and started yanking at her ties again. Moldy road kill lowered itself with a growl and stabbed the hand clean with the sharpened stick.

Her toenails and toes were one mass, two little battering rams sticking out of a new pair of jeans. Her flannel was stained with gore, worn backwards like an apron. Her shoulders hunched and bubbles popped in her open mouth. She held the boy's hand under an arm and stabbed at the stump, dark clumped tendrils of hair shaking from her huge head.

Dina saw that where the hand should be was only a protrusion, like a single large knuckle in front of the wrist. A sharpened broom handle was above it, tied to her forearm. She tried to force the nub of her arm into the base of the hand. Libby lost her hold and dropped it again. She looked over at Dina. Her leg appeared to twitch. The hand pulped beneath her battering ram foot as she moved toward Dina.

"What are you going to do? Libby! *What are you going to do?*"

The mold and road kill stink brushed past, out of sight. Libby grabbed something off the ground and returned to stand in front of Dina. She slipped a black drinking cup over her right forearm. A large fork was buried in the bottom of it. Broom handle on the left, she worked it under the binding on Dina's wrist.

Screaming realization, her second, much louder scream, one of pain. Bubbles popped on Libby's teeth. Her shoulders twisted toward the ground and Dina's wrist broke.

"Wrong! Wrong Libby!"

Popping bubbles became a burping chitter, squealing as she vanished.

The pain, the smell… Bile burned its way up and out her nose. Eyes roving under dark eyelids sought a less painful position. Dina strained to hear through the throbbing.

She recognized a sound, the *thwack* of Uncle Taylor's machete as he cleared a path up from the pond. She felt pressure on her numb hands and lifted her head.

"She watches them," Taylor said, lining up his wide blade to saw her free. "She thinks they wear costumes to make fun of her. I told her she was just being silly." He stopped sawing. "Did you see her new outfit? I got it for her."

Dina started coughing. *I don't care I don't care! Get me loose - hurry and cut my hands free!*

The binding popped. She crossed her arms as she fell away from the tree. He caught her, broken hand slapping into him. Her eyes appeared to sink in, darkening with blood sucked from her face.

Taylor picked her up, careful to keep her arms folded. 'She didn't mean it. Truly."

Dina hated the arms around her, hated the gratitude she felt. Hated that she couldn't take her cheek from his shoulder and tell him to fuck off.

Hated that her ass hanging below his arm was cold and she couldn't stop shaking.

She spit out a piece of her tongue. It clung to her lip. Spasms made her feet kick up, her neck lock into place, but she managed to look up and thank him with a smile.

He smiled back. The machete chopped midway through his forehead, the blade's tip leaking on her, and he continued to smile.

Marsh Madness

The heron stalked through the flooded marsh, eyes intent on movement below the muddy surface. Beak aimed like a javelin. It stopped, poised to strike. Patient.

The heron flinched before it burst out of the water, thrust from its huge wings leaving a mist like a jet's contrail as it soared to a safe height over the maze of marsh islands.

Out of the haze of fog drifting over the water emerged a man. Behind him, as if he had bore a tunnel through the thick gloom, were woods with ancient oak trees twisting out into the bayou. Long tendrils of dull gray moss snaking down to the mud seemed to vibrate with a dissonant buzz; hundreds of thousands of insects clung to the trees and brush along the bank, belting out a chorus that was randomly broken up by disturbances in the water.

Hunched over, dull gray beard hanging like moss from a sun-weathered face, the man blazed a trail of silence, stepping through the muck with a heron's patience. His eyes, black and stretched wide, had an unnatural gleam in the twilight.

An alligator hide rifle case was slung across his back, one hand holding the butt close to his flank, silencing its movement and that of his rubber waders. With his other hand he pushed aside sharp blades of grass that would have sliced into most people's skin.

He came to the edge of the marsh island and stilled himself. Standing tall, a scarecrow overlooking a huge field of dead corn stalks, his eyes shifted to the left as theme park music began playing in the far distance. A ferris wheel stood above the fog bank, lights from several small rides glaring up at it, giving the entire fairgrounds a faint glow. The high pitched, tinny notes penetrated the thick gloom, floating along with it.

The man bared his black gums in that direction for a moment. Deep wrinkles spread from his eyes and mouth. Absently, he rubbed his ear; a twisted, misshapen scar ran right through it.

A dog barked. The man's head turned forward in a blink, wrinkles deepening with a smile. Across the narrow channel was a large dog standing on a low wooden pier. A golden retriever. Behind the dog, on top of a hill, a dark gray mist shrouded a small mobile home. A breeze pushed out of the woods, momentarily showing a porch, a yellow light struggling to illuminate steps. A swing set, barbeque grill and trampoline were haphazardly placed in a large overgrown yard that sloped down to disappear into the high tide.

Claws ticked and scrambled over broken, failing planks. The dog barked at the water. A wave of silence spread rapidly throughout the marsh. The insects started up again. The dog's panting could be heard clearly across the channel.

The object of the dog's interest was three feet below the end of the pier. Sticking up like an old stump was the head of a bull alligator. The dog, unafraid, seemed to play a game familiar between the two. The barking, clawing and loud panting continued. Around the man frogs had joined the bugs, quieting after barks, as if considering how to reply and join in their game.

"Mario! Mario! Dummy. Get away from there." A small boy materialized in the mist at the top of the yard. A screen door creaked and slammed on the trailer. He ran down to the pier, stopped and whistled, clapped his hands. "Come here, boy. *Mario!*"

The retriever glanced at the boy, tongue lolling. Started wagging his tail. His head swivelled back to the alligator, mouth opening, closing, tip of his tongue wiggling with each pant. He barked again, pawed the pier. Bounced up and down, darted from side to side.

The man hadn't moved. He observed the alligator, peripherally tracking the boy and dog.

"Stupid dog! Come on. We're not supposed to play on the pier. Mom's gonna yell at us." He wrung his hands, chewing on his lip.

Mario kept barking and wagging at the alligator. The boy stepped carefully onto the pier, looked over his shoulder at the trailer, then ran to the end of the pier, leaping a jagged hole. His sneakers thumped to a stop, arms encircling Mario's neck. "Come *on*... What are you do-ing?" He looked down into the water. Wide-set emotionless eyes looked back at him. "Whoa! Crud! The alligator - !"

The dog turned to lick the boy, rear end wagging, and threw him from his feet. He shouted as his hands and chin banged hard on the planks. His shoes splashed in the water, legs sliding in. The alligator's head disappeared in a swirl of black.

The man moved quickly. Grabbing the top of the rifle case he unsnapped it, slid out a crossbow and unfolded the arms, locking them. Loaded a bolt. Brought it to his shoulder, aiming through a high-powered scope at the boy's legs.

"Mario!" All the boy's breath burst from him in a single scream. Around the man the marsh creatures scattered into the grass or water. The boy tore at the planks with his tiny fingers, shoes thudding into the water behind him.

The dog wore a puzzled expression. He chuffed, pawed the pier in front of the boy. Then he stretched and bit the collar of the boy's shirt, jerked and snatched him back onto the pier. The boy's shoes cleared right as the alligator popped up under them.

"Whoa! *Shoot!* Whoa! WHOA!" The boy staggered, gripping his shirt, pushing at Mario until he let go.

The big dog abruptly spun and ran off the pier.

The screen door slapped shut from the trailer and a tall sandy haired woman in jeans and flip-flops walked down to the water gesturing with a hair brush. "God-*damnit,* Sam! Really? I told you to not play by the water, and *specifically* not on the pier. And your freaking clothes are wet? Get your ass in the house and get changed! You're going to be late for the bus." She stuck the brush in a back pocket. Whistled loudly, clapped her hands. "Mario! Let's go, boy. Get your ass in the house! You better not be wet, too."

Mario barked and waggled, looking at the woman. Then he bound up the yard and raced past her.

The woman turned to follow her chastened son and the man aimed the scope at her ass. His lips peeled back, blackened gums catching light that darkened them further, lines branching from the corners of his eyes blending into single deep furrows. Jeans stretched over hips, jeans that dug into buttocks.

The man's finger caressed the weapon's trigger.

The stump appeared in the water again. This time where the yard met the water. The dog zoomed past the woman and boy, barking up a storm.

The man tracked the alligator as it moved slowly towards the yard, crosshairs centered just behind its eyes. Mario, bounding downhill, tongue lolling in a toothy smile, barked his I'm-a-Good-Dog-Let's-Play bark. As he came to a sudden stop, the man brought the crossbow up slightly and shot the dog in the front leg.

Gravity and momentum were against the big dog.

He pitched over into the bayou.

The stump vanished. The dog never surfaced.

The splash made Sam and the woman stop and turn around. They didn't see Mario. The woman frowned. The boy looked alarmed. When Mario didn't respond to their calls Sam ran back to the pier. The woman followed, flip-flops slapping hard against her feet.

The man took aim at her chest, shirt straining against her swaying breasts. His finger moved faster, though still gently, over the trigger.

"Well, where the hell is he?" The woman planted her feet, fists on hips. "Mario!" She demanded for Sam to find his dog and get his ass to the bus stop, wet clothes and all.

Sam, completely bewildered, looked from the pier to the water. Looked at his mom and shrugged. He squinted at the woods. Leaned over and peered intently through the fog, at the marsh across the channel.

He gasped and jerked upright. A sob caught in his throat as his eyes moved back to the pier. To the water.

He turned toward his mom. "The alligator, Mom. *The alligator!*"

"The alligator? What about the alligator?" The woman muttered 'Shit' and walked down next to Sam. Frowned at the water. Her eyebrows lifted. She put a hand to her mouth. She almost said, *But that old 'gator and Mario are friends...* But Sam knew better, and so did she.

Sam took a deep, sharp breath and let out a wail that pierced deep into the bayou.

The heavy fog began lifting. A fresh breeze billowed Sam's wet pants as he clung to his mother's leg, sobbing.

The man's smile broadened to a full grin, tiny pinpoints of light refracting from his jet eyes and gums.

One eye closed and he looked through the scope once more. A dry suction emitted from his throat, tongue pressing into his top gum, unsticking.

Carnival music, louder now that the fog was lifting, tinkled on the breeze as the man studied the woman's backside again. She bent over to pick up her crying son and carried him up to the porch.

Made in the USA
Lexington, KY
06 June 2018